"Mr. Casas, do you know where you are?"

He tried to speak but nothing came out, so he nodded his head, which hurt enough to make him stop.

"We're going to get you some water, okay? I want you to try and take a sip for me."

A straw appeared in his vision and after a few attempts, he managed to get enough down him to soothe his throat a little.

"Okay," the man said, Javier recognizing the man's voice from before. "Let's try that again. Do you know where you are?"

"Yes," Javier replied.

"Do you know what brought you here?"

He narrowed his eyes, trying to make his mouth say the words in his mind. He was on the brink of forcing the answer from his lips when the man fired another question at him.

"Can you tell me what the last thing you remember is?"

He frowned, the weight of expectation in the air different from the previous questions. His gaze flickered around the room—his mother, sister, the doctor and the nurse—but snagged on the doorway.

"Emily."

Pippa Roscoe lives in Norfolk near her family and makes daily promises to herself that this is the day she'll leave the computer to take a long walk in the countryside. She can't remember a time when she wasn't dreaming about handsome heroes and innocent heroines. Totally her mother's fault, of course—she gave Pippa her first romance to read at the age of seven! She is inconceivably happy that she gets to share those daydreams with you all. Follow her on Twitter, @pipparoscoe.

Books by Pippa Roscoe

Harlequin Presents

Rumors Behind the Greek's Wedding
Playing the Billionaire's Game

The Diamond Inheritance

Terms of Their Costa Rican Temptation
From One Night to Desert Queen
The Greek Secret She Carries

The Royals of Svardia

Snowbound with His Forbidden Princess
Stolen from Her Royal Wedding
Claimed to Save His Crown

Visit the Author Profile page
at Harlequin.com for more titles.

Pippa Roscoe

THE WIFE THE SPANIARD NEVER FORGOT

HARLEQUIN
PRESENTS

Recycling programs
for this product may
not exist in your area.

ISBN-13: 978-1-335-58409-0

The Wife the Spaniard Never Forgot

Copyright © 2022 by Pippa Roscoe

For questions and comments about the quality of this book,
please contact us at CustomerService@Harlequin.com.

Harlequin Enterprises ULC
22 Adelaide St. West, 41st Floor
Toronto, Ontario M5H 4E3, Canada
www.Harlequin.com

Printed in U.S.A.

THE WIFE THE SPANIARD NEVER FORGOT

For Nic, thank you for the friendship, wine and trip down memory lane that planted the seed for this story. (There is no such thing as too many Aperol Spritzes!)

And to the beautiful family holiday that helped it grow. Javi, I hope I've done Frigiliana justice!

xx

CHAPTER ONE

JAVIER CASAS LEFT the extravagance of In Venum—Madrid's newest and hottest night-club—two marble steps at a time, rubbing at his tired eyes. *That's what happens when you push yourself too hard*, taunted the warning his closest friend had uttered only days ago. Javier huffed. Santi was filming his latest blockbuster hit during the day and finishing post-production on another in the evening—he was hardly one to talk.

'Casas!' a predatory female voice called, halting his steps. He couldn't claim not to have heard her in deserted Spanish streets at two o'clock in the morning, even though he was tempted.

He turned. She was two steps above him, but barely at eye level with his six-foot four-inch frame. Behind her, he caught the eye of the bouncer framing the door at the top of the steps and discreetly shook his head. Javier would deal with the woman himself. She'd managed to ignore all of his subtle and then not so subtle refusals so far that night, making the entire evening a practice in avoidance. He hadn't even wanted to come tonight, but he couldn't miss the grand opening for a bar that he owned forty-nine percent of—*silently.*

She reached out, red-nailed fingers gripping his shoulder. 'I thought that we could go somewhere.'

She licked her lips in a move she probably believed was sensual, but to Javier was deeply disturbing. The light from the club's entrance created a painfully bright aura around her, illuminating rather than disguising her ravenous desperation.

'You need to go home, Annalise.'

'There is a lot that I need, Javier, and I think you could help me with that.'

'Annalise—'

'I want your hands on me,' she whispered, leaning closer, and before he could stop her she had her finger on the zip of his trousers. He cursed, twisting free of her clutches.

'Basta ya!' But she didn't stop. He clasped her hands to keep them from grabbing other parts of his anatomy and stepped back as she tried to press herself against him. 'I'm *mar-*

ried, Annalise,' he growled between gritted teeth.

She rolled her eyes. 'You are never seen with anyone on your arm, so we all know that's just a ruse. Unless you keep her locked up in your house and never let her out?'

He frowned, his brain trying to work out who 'we' was and whether she was joking or not.

'You could keep *me* locked up, if you like?'

He didn't have time for this. His driver was waiting and he had a meeting in five hours. He didn't bother responding. Instead he nodded to the man by the entrance, who appeared and gently prised her from him.

'Make sure she gets back to wherever she's staying safely,' he ordered over his shoulder, knowing it would be followed without question, and continued towards the car waiting for him.

'Don't look at me like that,' Javier groused when he reached Esteban. His driver's expression hadn't changed a bit, but wry amusement came off him in waves.

'Didn't say a thing, sir,' his chauffeur replied.

Once settled in the back of the car, Javier checked his phone for the upcoming day's meetings, making sure that everything was on track to start bang on seven a.m. He scanned the two hundred emails his personal assistant had already filtered and checked the family message group he had with his half-sister and his mother—but neither distracted him from the sudden unwanted thoughts about the wife he hadn't seen for six years.

Angry with himself for not having more restraint, he pulled up the newspaper article that had been published last month. *More Than Just a Pretty Paintbrush—UK's hottest new interior designer making waves.* He scanned the puff piece that was more patronising than it was illuminating. He'd read it almost ten times now and each time his gaze snagged on the photograph of the woman who had left him on an evening that should have changed their lives for very different reasons.

The black and white picture showed her in a white shirt, holding a cup of coffee, looking towards the camera as if she had a delicious secret to share. Her eyes sparkled in a way he barely recognised and it infuriated him beyond belief that the way her hands cupped the mug concealed her ring finger.

Did she still wear it?

The car slowed and took an unfamiliar turn. Javier frowned, catching the flicker of his driver's eyes in the rear-view mirror.

'Badly signed roadworks. We're going to have to—'

The entire world shifted in an explosion of screaming metal and shattering glass. Swept up in a wave that crushed the confines of the car, Javier found himself upside down, choking on a vicious pain in his side. Time jerked back and forth between shocking speed and incomprehensible slowness. A piercing light cut between blue and white, making him wince as a figure he couldn't be sure was actually there knelt in glass. Blood dripped into his eye, but he couldn't move his hand to wipe it away.

Something bad had happened. Something awful even, but he couldn't understand what. He caught words like 'hospital' and the oddly irritating reassurance that everything would be okay. To the left he saw his phone, a shatter across the screen and, beneath the broken shards, an image of Emily about to tell him her secret, just before everything went black.

'Okay, that's it, ladies and gentlemen, time to leave.'

'But, boss—'

'It's one in the morning. Don't you have bars to drink in? Dates to go on? Homes to get to?' Emily teased. She loved her small team; they were eager and hungry, just like she was, but she knew how quickly hunger could morph into burnout and a healthy team was as important to her as their income.

'But we haven't finalised the tiles in the bathroom, the colours for the third and fourth bedrooms, and—'

'It can all wait until tomorrow.' She gathered up the coffee cups, cutting them off from the only thing that had kept them going this long, and one by one her two designers, one architect and her much loved assistant made their way out of the door.

Once alone, Emily sighed. They'd done good work on the Northcote project in the Cotswolds but the restaurant in San Antonio was niggling. It was still early days but she hadn't found *the thing* yet. And Emily would continue to be unsettled until she found *the thing* that brought the project together.

It had always been like that. Ever since she'd finished the evening course with the Design Institute. Returning from Spain, full of heartache, with nowhere to live and no idea what to do, had been awful. Until Francesca, her best friend, had invited Emily to stay in her home while she went travelling with her boyfriend. The only proviso was that Emily 'oversaw' the renovation of the kitchen/diner. Desperate for a distraction from the hope that her husband would come for her—that her sudden and shocking absence might finally make him notice her—Emily had first shadowed the interior designer and then become more of a project manager, coordinating the revolving door of tradespeople.

Through the months of the renovation, Emily had realised Javier wasn't coming for her. That the man she loved with a desperation that had almost ruined her had accepted her absence from his life as easily as a change in the weather. The devastation had very nearly ruined her, but as Fran's project came to a close the interior designer—Maggie—had encouraged her to take the Design Institute's course, insisting that Emily had an 'eye for it'.

So Emily had thrown herself into the world of interior design. She'd studied at night, working with Maggie during the day, learning from anyone she met. And when she had taken on her first job? It had been terrifying, with steep learning curves and intense hard work, but it had been a resounding success. And word of mouth had soon spread. People loved Emily's dedication and ability to reach beyond what her clients wanted to what they *needed*. And that thing that held an entire project together? Identifying it had become an integral part of Emily's process, but one that couldn't be forced.

Needing a little decompression time before she went to bed, she opened the fridge and poured herself a glass of white Rioja. Leaning against the kitchen's countertop, she relished the silence of the large warehouse floor in Bermondsey that was all hers. The office, where scattered paper and laptops lay on a long industrial table, was partitioned off from her living area by wide factory-style windows and carefully placed planters bursting with greenery.

A sprawling white fluffy rug lay in front of an L-shaped sofa that was more comfortable than her bed. The magazine, open at the article she'd done last month, shimmered beneath the overhead light and Emily cringed. They said there was no such thing as bad publicity, but the puff piece had been written by a man who had sacrificed integrity for alliteration, and had focused on her appearance rather than her talent. But she couldn't deny that they had seen an increase in traffic on their website.

They were already beyond a healthy capacity, Emily knew, but she couldn't resist the lure of security that more work offered. *'Just hire more staff.'* The directive came with a typically Spanish shoulder-shrug. *'I'll give you the money.'*

The voice, sounding very much like her estranged husband, failed to grasp how important it was to Emily that she ran her business on *her* terms. But then he'd always done that— seen things the way *he* saw them, not bending for anything or anyone. So, no. She'd make it work with what she had until she knew absolutely that she could afford to expand.

She took a sip of wine and looked out of the window and down onto the deserted south London streets. Small boutique coffee shops punched above their weight next to international chains. Luxury apartments stared down defiant Victorian terraces and artist studios filled the docks next to Michelin starred restaurants. It was chaos in all its London beauty. But, for all the affection she felt for the area and the success she'd achieved with her career, Emily couldn't deny that something was missing. It had been creeping up on her in the last few years, as if, now that professionally she was beginning to feel secure, a new need, a new yearning was on the horizon. A more personal one.

Placing the glass of wine on the windowsill, she looked at the simple gold band on her ring finger. They'd been in such a hurry to wed, as if, even then, they'd worried that time might change their minds. She'd known that Javier would have preferred something grander, the ring *and* the ceremony. But she'd been quietly happy, the plain gold band more meaningful than a precious jewel that wouldn't have suited her at all.

She splayed her fingers, indecision warring deep within her. As if this were a line in the sand, as if removing it would be an act she couldn't take back. Gritting her teeth, she took off the ring, placing it beside her glass on the window ledge. She inhaled through the feeling of unease and took a sip of wine to cover the taste of tension on her tongue. She shook out her hands and flexed her fingers, hoping to dispel the sudden and intense feeling of *absence*.

Her phone's ringtone made her jump—the sound unusual and alarming at this time of night. She caught the Spanish area code in the unfamiliar number flashing on the screen as she went to answer it and a sense of foreboding cut into her breathing, quick and sharp. Responding to the caller, she confirmed that yes, she was Mrs Casas, and then the glass of wine slipped from her numb fingers and shattered on the floor.

Pain.

It gripped his head like a vice and when he breathed it was as if the devil himself had thrust a red-hot poker between his ribs. A lifelong habit had him stifling the groan that threatened to escape his throat. Javier knew he wasn't alone, and he *really* wanted to be alone.

Earlier—he couldn't say exactly when— he thought he'd heard his mother, which had been, unsurprisingly, enough to send him back under. Now he tried to hold onto the voices; a man was speaking in hushed but frustrated tones. So his mother *was* there.

Javier breathed as deeply as he dared and nearly cried out loud from the pain in his chest. Somewhere in the room a monitor beeped noisily, halting the conversation until the sound returned to a steadier rhythm and the voices resumed.

Why couldn't he remember what had happened?

He was in a hospital, that much was clear.

'He should be locked up!' his mother cried, shrill and overly loud. For a moment, Javier wondered if Renata was talking about him.

'He has spoken to the police, assisted them in their investigation and is not currently under any suspicion,' the confident male voice explained.

'But how can that be?' Renata demanded. 'He was driving!'

Esteban. They'd had an accident? Was Esteban okay? The beeping monitor increased in speed again, frustrating Javier beyond belief.

He wanted to ask but he couldn't seem to make his mouth do what he wanted it to.

'It is clear to everyone that it was not his fault and he will be discharged later today.'

'While my son stays here?' There was a pause, as if the room's occupants tried to fathom Renata's illogical response to the different injuries sustained by the two men. 'I want to talk to your boss.' His mother was practically screeching now.

'I am Chief of Surgery.'

'Who is your boss?'

'Mrs Casas, why don't we go to my office?'

'I will not leave my son!' The outrage in her voice was horribly familiar. That, more than any pain, brought a cold sweat to his brow. Renata was difficult, truly difficult, and the only way he'd found to successfully navigate her personality was to put distance between them. He would have put the moon between them had it not been for his sister Gabi. His jumbled brain threw up a memory from his childhood that would have nearly buckled him had he been standing.

Please, Mamá, it hurts.

He went back under.

The next time he woke the sounds were slightly different, there was a silence in the room that encouraged him to risk a peek through heavy-lidded eyes. The bright white disorientated him for a moment and he closed them before the agony pressing into his brain became too much. But the quiet gave him enough space to think. He had been out—In Venum. The launch. He'd been there and…

I want your hands on me…

An unpleasant shiver ran through him at the memory. He'd got to the car with Esteban and…the roadworks. Javier braced, remembering the moment of impact, the way the world had swung and swayed. Blood in his eye…

'Who is Emily?' an unfamiliar female voice asked.

The monitor trilled again as his heart jumped awkwardly at the question.

'He's been saying her name over and over.'

Had he?

'No one,' his mother replied, sharp as steel and just as cutting.

For a moment his brain went blank and he thought he might have blacked out again, but his senses were still full of the room.

'Mother!' his sister said, outraged. 'Emily is his wife,' his sister explained to the stranger.

Anger filled him, tension cording his neck and fists. His wife was a lot of things, but most definitely never *no one*. No, he hadn't been surprised that Renata had been unhappy with his choice of wife—an English girl, barely twenty, who couldn't speak a word of Spanish. But his wife was *family*.

'That girl was nothing more than a—'

He forced his eyes open and whatever his mother had been about to say was cut off by the sudden flurry of activity around his bed. Fingers prodded and poked and someone shook his shoulders, not gently enough for him to ignore but not rough enough to hurt, tying him to the room when all he wanted to do was go back to the black.

'Mr Casas? Can you hear me?'

The woman was insistent and he raised his hand to ward her off, but his arm didn't move more than an inch. His throat thickened with frustration and he wanted to howl. Goddammit! Why wasn't his body doing what it was supposed to?

'Mr Casas, do you know where you are?'

He tried to speak but nothing came out, so nodded, which hurt enough to make him stop.

'We're going to get you some water, okay? I want you to try and take a sip for me.'

A straw appeared in his vision and, after a few attempts, he managed to get enough down him to soothe his throat a little.

'Okay,' the man said—Javier recognised the

voice from before. 'Let's try that again. Do you know where you are?'

'Yes,' Javier managed.

'Do you know what brought you here?'

He narrowed his eyes, trying to make his mouth say the words in his mind. He was on the brink of forcing the answer from his lips when the man fired another question at him.

'Can you tell me the last thing you remember?'

Javier frowned, the weight of expectation in the air different to the previous questions. His gaze flickered around the room—his mother, sister, the doctor and the nurse—but snagged on the doorway.

'Emily.'

Standing in the doorway to his hospital room, Emily was stunned by what she saw. In a pale blue medical gown, attached to monitors, Javier lay propped up, a vicious bruise slashed across his cheek, a cut marring the planes of his proud forehead, but it was the paleness of his skin that really shocked her. Javier was *never* pale.

Through a crazy dash to the airport and a nerve-racking flight, Emily had told herself that Javier was fine. Because there wasn't a reality in which Javier was anything other than a truly powerful force of nature. She could only believe that there had been some kind of misunderstanding. But the two and a half hour flight had given her too much time to think.

She'd tried not to read too much into the fact that she was still his next of kin, hating the way it made her heart leap. Because it was too familiar. Too similar to the hope she'd nursed in the first months after she'd returned from Spain. And then, in the blink of an eye, the time she'd been back had eclipsed the entire time she'd known him, and he'd not come for her.

She'd arrived at the hospital and found her way to the private ward, nearly passing the room completely when the sight of him had pulled her up short. Her heart in her mouth, she'd listened for his answers to the doctor's questions, needing to know that he was okay. He *had* to be okay. Her thumb had reached to stroke the ring she'd retrieved just before leaving her apartment when she'd heard her name on his lips.

Her eyes snapped to his, frozen in place by the intensity of his gaze until—

'Amnesia!' his mother screamed and Emily, tired and wrung-out, rolled her eyes. She thought she saw a glimmer of a smirk from Javier but a blink and it was gone.

The doctor saw her standing in the doorway and nodded his acknowledgement.

'My baby has amnesia! Do something.'

'Mrs Casas.' The doctor's firm tone snapped Renata to attention and she allowed him to gesture her out of the hospital room into the corridor, where she turned an ugly shade of red the moment she caught sight of her son's wife.

'I don't know what *she* is doing here,' Renata rushed out in rapid Spanish.

'She is Javier's next of kin.' He turned to Emily, seemingly unaware that to call her 'Mrs Casas' in front of Renata would incite violence. 'You *are* Mr Casas's wife?' he asked in Spanish. Emily was about to answer but his mother interrupted.

'She doesn't speak Spanish.' The disdain in the older woman's tone was unmistakable.

Emily bit back a retort. No, she hadn't spoken Spanish at the beginning of her relationship with Javier but she had made the effort to learn it, even after she'd returned to England when she'd thought she might still need it.

Renata stared straight at the doctor as if trying to cut Emily out of her line of sight and Emily was surprised it still hurt. His mother had never been anything but barely tolerant of her presence at the best of times, and this was *not* the best of times.

Deciding not to challenge Renata's statement, she allowed the doctor to bring her up to speed in English. The accident had caused a fracture of three ribs, some very nasty cuts and bruises but miraculously no broken bones. Most of his injuries were considered 'superficial', leaving Emily a little concerned by their definition. Over the doctor's shoulder she saw Javier arguing with the nurse about the electrodes he was trying to remove from his chest.

Taking advantage of his distraction, her hungry gaze consumed the rest of him. His massive frame looked almost comically large in the bed, but there was nothing funny about the collage of bruises across skin that was a shocking shade of grey. From the very first moment she'd met Javier, he'd been an explosion of life and colour—a vivid virility mixed with a charm that bordered on lethal, one that she'd surrendered to utterly and irrevocably.

The moment she felt Javier's focus shift from the nurse to her, she looked back to the doctor. Javier's attention might have been as gentle as a caress but it was as hot as a flame and just as dangerous.

'You are concerned about his memory?' she asked, unaware that she had interrupted Renata.

Both she and the doctor ignored the older

woman's huff of outrage. 'Yes. He has a concussion. Scans show a little bruising that will go down in time, but we will need to run more tests to know if there is cause for significant concern.'

She forced herself to meet Javier's eyes through the window to his room, but what she saw in his gaze stopped her thoughts. Calculation. Determination. There was absolutely *nothing* hindering Javier Casas's mental processing. But the doctor didn't seem to see what she saw.

'What does this mean? If it is…amnesia?' she asked.

'It will depend on how much he remembers, *what* he remembers. But, in rehabilitation terms, the main goal is to make him comfortable and keep things familiar without forcing a return of memories.'

Emily tried to get at what the doctor wasn't saying, but knew it was pointless until they knew more. 'Run your tests.'

The next few hours passed in a blur. Emily waited outside the room while the tests were conducted, which was fine by Javier's mother. His half-sister Gabi came out and sat next to her without speaking. Emily was surprised when the young woman she remembered as a beautiful teenager took her hand and held on tight. It was as if neither wanted to say anything until they knew what was going on.

What would she do? Whatever the outcome, Javier would need help. Maybe he'd hire someone to stay with him? She'd read that he'd moved into an apartment in Madrid, ashamed by how greedily she'd consumed information about him in the gossip columns over the years. He'd be fine, she reassured herself like a mantra, over and over and over. That was all she needed to know and then she could leave. If she was lucky, she might make it back to London having only missed a day.

But...she knew that was a lie. Six years might have passed since she had last seen her husband, but she felt it. Time was up. There would be no more hiding from her marriage to this Spanish billionaire. An icy finger was tripping its way down her spine when the doctor came out, looking a little puzzled but hopeful.

'Mr Casas is doing well. Cognitively he's retained all normal function. However, the last few years are almost a blank to him. At the moment, his brain is struggling to cope with the injury, so the goal is to create a peaceful and quiet environment. To reduce any further risk, it's going to be important that you are with him at all times. There may be periods where he gets frustrated with his rehabilitation, where he asks the same thing repeatedly. It will be wearing and difficult, so it's important that you have support and help too.'

'Me? Why would I need support?' Emily's tired mind was taking too long to catch up.

'Because you will be allowed to take him home in a few days and you'll be caring for him, no?'

Her head snapped to Javier, his gaze on her steady and waiting.

Emily tuned out the doctor's words as she realised what it meant. What was expected of her. What Javier had forced her into. It was a *knowing*. Deep in her gut, and low in her heart. There was no amnesia. The look in his eyes told her that he remembered everything. Worse, it was the anger simmering in that gaze. An anger that she had never seen before, but knew categorically had been put there by her departure six years before.

Her husband, it seemed, was playing games and it infuriated her. Was this his way of punishing her for leaving all those years ago? His final act of revenge? Oh, she had no doubt that he had cast himself the innocent in his mind. But Javier Casas—the man who was *never* wrong—had made a fatal mistake this time. She was no longer the unconfident young bride of before. She had changed and if he wanted to wilfully and carelessly mess with her life then it was only fair that she do the same.

Entering the room, she went to his bedside, taking his hand in hers. For a second, she thought she saw a flare in his irises, the surprise contact shocking them both. But this wasn't her caring husband, the man who had swept her off her feet at nineteen and offered her the world. No. It was the man who had shown her the world only on his terms. And now she was going to do the same. She leaned forward, sweeping his thick dark hair from his forehead in seeming affection, his skin warm beneath the cold of her fingers, and leaned to his ear.

'If you think for one second,' she whispered, 'that I believe a word of this, you are sorely mistaken. And you *will* regret it.'

CHAPTER TWO

EMILY LEFT THE HOSPITAL, saying that she needed time to prepare for Javier's return. She had meant with regard to their house in Frigiliana, but in reality she needed that time for herself. Because if things went the way she thought they would, then these would be her last days as Mrs Javier Casas.

Emily pushed against the iron gate that opened into a small courtyard at the front of the house. The slash of fuchsia bougainvillea was stunning against the brilliant white of the wall, but the build-up of leaves and bits of rubbish blown in by the wind hinted at a neglect Emily felt in her soul.

She had *loved* this house. With an enthusiasm and fervour that had been all-consuming, she had spent hours filling it with her early forays into decorating, unable to quite believe that this was theirs. It was a far cry from the small two-up, two-down in Morden she had moved to when her mother had married Steven. Her stepfather liked things practical, and practical usually involved beige in one form or another. But this, she thought as she shook out the front door key, this had been her *home*.

For less than a nanosecond she paused, key half turned, wondering what she would find on the other side of the door. Would there be a woman's shirt in the bedroom? Lipstick, toothbrush…? But that didn't ring true. No matter what had passed or not passed between them, Javier had a moral line that would not be crossed. No. He would have remained faithful, but from fidelity to his vows rather than her.

She pushed against the door and was hit by a wave of nostalgia so strong and so powerful it rocked her where she stood. Even the smell was the same. Thoughtlessly she put her keys on the small side table to the right of the door as if she'd last done it only yesterday and walked towards the dining room table they'd spent two argumentative hours and five thousand euros on. The price was still inconceivable to her but she couldn't deny how stunning it was. Carved from a single piece of oak, it was the colour of honey and warm to the touch, no matter what time of year. Even now she couldn't resist reaching out to run her hand along it. They had feasted in this room, laughed until they had cried, they'd even made love on this table, so caught up in their desire for each other that plates had smashed against the floor. She'd bet that if she looked down she would still see the stain from the red wine they'd spilt that night. Instead, she looked into her memories and saw herself sitting here night after night alone, as she'd waited for her husband to come home, one lonely dinner after another.

The stairs in the left corner led up to the master and spare bedrooms, but she chose to follow the hallway on the right that led through to a stunning living area with floor-to-ceiling windows and a view that literally stole her breath. Although the house was a stone's throw from the heart of Frigiliana, it was situated at the top of the road that led away from the cobbled streets and lively restaurants and down to the bottom of a large gorge. Clinging to the edge of town, their home looked out onto the deep green foliage of the other side of the gorge and, if lucky, you could spot the occasional mountain goat.

Emily had spent hours staring out at that view. She had never seen such vibrant greens, set against a blue that no man could recreate. To the right of the room was a small white and green tiled patio that overlooked the lower level and swimming pool. Her mind threw memory after memory at her. She heard her own shocked cry turn to laughter as Javier swept her up fully clothed and jumped into the water with her. Laughter that had turned quickly into moans of delight and pleasure as he had peeled off her clothing piece by piece until there was nothing left between them.

Standing there now, looking down at the pool, Emily wondered if that had been the last time she'd made love to her husband, feeling that there was something so incredibly sad about not knowing. Her heart aching, she turned back to the room. Nothing had changed, she thought, as she looked up at the large rough-hewn white walls. A blank canvas she'd thought she'd paint her future on. A future that had never come to pass.

He hadn't changed a single thing, but the entire house was clean of dust—as if someone came at least once a week to air it. And it made her unaccountably angry. Angry that her departure had cost him nothing like the years of agony it had caused her. Angry that he had not changed a single thing, while everything in her life had been thrown wildly off-course.

And he'd done it again. His 'memory loss' had upended her entire life, disrupting her work schedule, and for what? So that he could have fun at her expense? So that she would return to his bedside and nurse him back to health as if nothing had happened? As punishment?

Well, a lot had happened and while some things had changed—she had built a successful career and found a self-confidence she had desperately needed—some things hadn't. And one of those things was access to their joint account. And suddenly Emily wanted to see just how much he *couldn't* remember.

Javier fisted his hand as the car took another corner on the winding road leading to Frigiliana, ignoring the concerned glances the driver flicked his way in the rear-view mirror. It didn't matter that Javier knew every twist and turn on this road by heart—he probably could have driven blindfolded—but the moment he felt his stomach lurch he was back in the car that had been hit so hard and fast by a truck whose driver hadn't seen the poorly lit sign for the roadworks it had rolled the car mid-air and landed Javier and Esteban upside down.

The moment his sister had enticed his mother away from his hospital room, he'd reached for his phone and called his driver. Thankfully he was okay, aside from feeling guilty and fearful, no doubt thanks to Renata. It had taken almost ten minutes and more energy than Javier had expected to reassure Esteban that he was still employed.

The moment he'd ended the call, the *policía* arrived. The two uniformed men had been quick to assure him that he was under no suspicion and that they just wanted to know what he remembered from that night. Reluctantly admitting that he had been less than truthful with his family and doctor about his memory, he'd told the officers what he knew, refusing even for a second to put Esteban in a vulnerable position.

The officer had nodded without even a blink. 'Happens more than you think.'

They'd departed, leaving Javier wondering just how often billionaires faked amnesia.

Javier wasn't entirely sure why he'd gone along with it. Initially it hadn't been intentional. He'd seen Emily standing there and his mother had misunderstood. But the fact that Emily *was* there, that she *had* come... It had shocked him into silence. She looked exactly like she had in the picture in that magazine. Older, more assured, with just a little hint of cynicism that hadn't been there before. *Before* she'd left him without a thought or second look.

Then the damn monitor had kicked off, happily declaring to the entire room just how much her presence affected his blood pressure. He'd nearly ripped off the electrodes then and there. But even he'd seen that she'd been as affected as he had.

And then had come the fire. Oh, it had been incredible to see. He'd always known it was there—she couldn't have been capable of the incendiary passion that had kept them in bed for the entire first week of their marriage otherwise. But she'd never let it so close to the surface.

If you think for one second that I believe a word of this...

In the back of the car closing the distance between him and Emily, Javier smiled. It was the powerful woman he'd always known her to be, but hadn't seen before. From the first moment he'd laid eyes on Emily, he'd fallen hard. It was the strangest thing—just *knowing* that this was the woman he'd marry, the woman he'd spend his life with. A knowing that had proved wrong. So utterly and incomprehensibly wrong it had threatened to shake the foundations of his sense of self.

So why had she come? She could have easily had the hospital contact Renata or Gabi instead. Yet she hadn't. And, judging by the time of her arrival, she must have been on the first flight out. Thinking back to the hospital, his first reaction had been one of shocking relief—and then such an intense state of confusion. Because she had left him, walked away from him without a word or a second glance, the memory of her abandonment making him want to lash out. To punish her. He had been tempted to allow this amnesia thing play out, curious as to how far he could push the wife who had abandoned him, but his conscience had overruled it. He'd known that he'd have to come clean with her the moment she'd left the hospital. He wasn't so much of a bastard as to completely upend her life to suit his own needs.

But he wouldn't have been discharged from hospital on his own, and he refused to convalesce at Renata's house. He rubbed at the scar on his collarbone. He knew exactly what kind of care he'd have received there. His stomach turned—this time not from the bend in the road, but the argument he'd had with her.

'A son should be with his mother.'

Not *Let me look after you*, or *Let's get you better*. Once again, as it always did, the world turned around Renata. His sister had shot him sympathetic looks, the siblings bonded by an understanding of their mother that no one else would ever share. He hated the idea of Gabi being subjected to Renata's tantrums, but when he'd asked her to come and live with him years earlier Gabi had rejected his offer, insisting that Renata needed her. Javier drew a deep breath. His mother's manipulations were extensive, but if she followed her usual pattern she'd be silent for at least a good few days. And then she'd be in touch as if nothing had happened, asking him for money.

Which gave him the time he needed to finally deal with Emily once and for all.

We all know that's just a ruse.' Annalise's accusation from before the accident ran through his mind.

Jaw clenched, hand fisted, Javier had ignored the past for too long and it couldn't be avoided any longer.

His phone rang just as the car navigated the roundabout and along the narrow cobbled road through the lower part of town. His assistant, aware of the true state of his memory, was convinced that one of Javier's bank accounts had been hacked.

'That is impossible,' he replied firmly, knowing just how much he paid to protect his considerable assets.

'Sir, no. I don't think it is, because in the

last three days nearly nine thousand euros has been spent.'

'Three days?' he repeated, his mind snagging on that rather than the amount of missing money.

'I'm sorry, sir. It's not an account that I've seen activity on before and because you were in hospital I—'

'The account number?'

Darien reeled off a series of digits Javier knew by heart. It was an account he co-signed and it hadn't been touched for years, even in the months before Emily had left Spain. He was about to ask Darien what the purchases were when the car turned down the winding road that led to the house he'd once shared with Emily and he began to suspect he knew *exactly* what the money had been spent on.

Emily bit her lip. She *might* have gone a little too far with the last of the purchases. She looked around the space she had spent three days and an inconceivable amount of money transforming. She nearly grimaced at the bright pink slash of colour from the two massive canvases she'd installed in the main room. But they weren't as bad as the five-foot ceramic parrot. Even with memory loss, Emily was sure Javier wouldn't believe that he'd allowed the monstrosity into the house.

It had been a terrifying waste of money and when she succeeded in getting Javier to admit that he was lying she would pay him back every penny. She might even use some of the things in future projects. The pieces themselves weren't terrible—parrot aside—just not right for the house at all. She was wondering whether she might be able to use some for the San Antonio project when she heard the crunch of tyres on gravel outside the house and a shiver ran down her spine. She was being silly, she thought as she fanned the sudden rush of heat to her cheeks. But now that he was near, she also felt a thrill of excitement—she was flirting with danger, taunting Javier. And it was the most alive she'd felt in months.

The sound of a car door closing cut through her thoughts as she fussed with the heavily—and quite horribly—laced linen tablecloth she had regrettably covered the beautiful table with. It had been strange to use her skills in interior design to cultivate chaos rather than calm and she blamed the jarring sense of aesthetics for why she jumped when she heard the knock on the door.

She opened the door and all her planned responses burnt to ash in the bright afternoon sun. *That* was what caused her to squint up at the man who filled the doorway, she told herself. Not the impact of seeing him standing there. Nostalgia, not desire, flooded her veins, bringing a flush to her skin and an extra beat to her heart.

But for just a moment she forgot. Forgot how, after the honeymoon period had worn off, she had spent far too many hours here alone while Javier worked all the hours God sent. Forgot how isolated and lost she had felt here with no friends and no easy way to make them, fearful that she'd become exactly what she had never wanted to become—a woman who lost herself to her husband, who was totally dependent on him, just like her mother had become on her husband.

Dressed in a white shirt and tan trousers, Javier looked nothing like the easy-going, charming boy she'd fallen in love with. There were hints of him, the self-confidence that had always bordered on arrogance, the stubborn determination that had seen him win any argument he'd wanted to...but there was more of the man now. In the breadth of his shoulders, the slight creases around his eyes, bracketing his mouth, even the few—*very* few—silver threads in his hair and stubble that added authority and experience and diminished nothing of the raw power that swept at her like an unending tide.

His thick dark hair was swept back from his forehead and the natural jut of his jaw that made him look almost perpetually defiant was both familiar and heartbreaking and she had the maddening urge to kiss him. To reach for him and pull him across the threshold by his shirt, just as she had done so many times in the first few months of their marriage. A flash of glitter in his eyes, the ever so slight tightening of his jaw, fired warning signals in her brain and with a primal sense of self-preservation she stepped back to let him pass into the house.

'Welcome home,' she said, her gaze fastened to his, searching his face for any sign of surprise that might betray him.

What. Had. She. Done?

The words sounded in his head, even as he broadened the smile on his lips purposely to disguise the utter horror that struck him. Hard. In the three seconds he'd allowed himself to take in everything he could see—and he could see a *lot*—he had to work harder than he ever had before to school his features.

'Well?' she asked, one foot tucked behind the other, a slight lean to her head that dared him to call her on the changes she'd made to their home.

He frowned, as if a little confused. 'Have you done something different?' he asked, looking around as if he meant the house. He turned back to Emily in time to see her leap on his statement, her mouth open and ready to accuse, but he pushed on before she could. 'It's your hair. It's shorter?'

The flash in her cobalt-blue gaze burned like lightning across the Alboran Sea. Fuming. She was fuming and, petty that he was, he kind of enjoyed it. After all, *madre de Dios*, she'd made their home abhorrent. He fought the urge to wince.

'Longer, actually,' she replied with a little growl that nearly made him smile.

He gestured to his head. 'I'm sorry, this memory thing. It's got me turned around.' The lie rolled off his tongue as easily as his wife seemed to have destroyed their home. He stalked over to where she leaned against the wall and his gaze flicked from an ugly linen tablecloth on what was possibly his favourite item of furniture through to the flashes of fuchsia in the living area that, frankly, scared the living daylights out of him.

He turned his attention back to the real threat. Emily looked pretty in a white shirt and denim jeans rolled up from the ankles, but it was the bare feet that poked and prodded at his memories—the way she used to giggle when he captured them in his hands, pressing kisses against the arch of her foot. The memory fired a familiar anger in him. One that cried out loud at her betrayal—at her abandonment. And, bastard that he was, he wanted to push her, taunt her with the only connection he knew still burned bright between them.

He leaned down towards her, crowding her personal space in a way he couldn't bring himself to feel guilt over. She craned her neck, staring up at him, watchful and wary, eyes becoming larger and larger, her pupils flaring under his attention as he bent towards her, so slowly that she had time to move, but so confident that she wouldn't. He felt it, the thickening of his blood, the slow burn that had never gone, no matter how long or how far apart they'd been. The warm scent of her skin teased him, pushing and pulling at desires he'd thought he'd long forgotten. As he drew even closer, her lips opened on a little gasp that he felt against his own before, at the last moment, he turned to press a kiss to her cheek.

The roil of his stomach muscles sliced at his ribs and he couldn't prevent the sharp inhale of pain. Anger turned to worry in the blink of an eye and she placed her hand on his arm, stopping him when he would have turned away.

'Are you okay?' Emily asked, genuine concern in her tone.

'Yes,' he said, dismissing her question despite the tidal wave of ache that brushed over him again and again, and the exhaustion that threatened to suffocate him. He'd never felt anything like it and he hated it. Hated the weakness in his body.

If he'd hesitated for even just a second he would have seen the hurt shimmering in the blue depths of her gaze as he closed himself off from her, but he didn't as he pushed himself through his own discomfort.

Awkwardly he made his way through to the living area, squinting to lessen the impact of the bright pink of the paintings Emily had brought into the room. He was sure they'd cost an obscene amount—partly because his wife had always had good taste, even when she was trying to make it bad, but also because he knew how much she'd spent in the last three days.

He sat down gracelessly on the new and deeply uncomfortable banquette seating covering the far wall, undeniably impressed by what Emily had achieved in just three days, but nevertheless ready to pay any financial amount required for the return of his sofa. The firm canvas cushion offered no respite from the tension and ache that was growing closer to pain by the second. When he finally lifted his gaze, he found himself staring down a five-foot white ceramic parrot.

His wife had been possessed by a demon.

The swift inhale thrust another needle into his lungs. He'd been ready to admit that he'd lied, even willing to apologise to her for having her come all this way and for interrupting her life. But this?

This was an act of war.

She was making changes to their house to *taunt* him, to force him to admit that he was lying. Well, she should have known better. Because Javier Casas did not lose and he was one hundred percent determined that soon, very soon, she would be begging, no, *pleading*, for mercy.

CHAPTER THREE

EMILY MIXED A salad dressing while trying to shake the horrible feeling that she'd got it all terribly wrong. He'd not said a thing, not reacted to any of the changes she'd made at all. And she was *sure* that the parrot would have done it.

Could he really have amnesia?

The only thing she hadn't missed was the way he'd tried to hide the pain he was in. Its shadow had whispered across his cheeks and she remembered well how much he had always hidden any sign of weakness. At the beginning of their relationship his stoicism had attracted her, but by the end she had resented it. The doctor had emailed her a list of the medication and the doses he would need over the next two weeks before they returned for a review, with instructions to contact him if she needed anything. She stifled a laugh. She needed a dictionary, a calculator and her own headache tablets.

Emily nibbled at the nail of the thumb on her right hand, unseeing of the feast she had gathered for dinner. She had, in fact, made him the meal he'd most hated from their time together, but that had been thrown into the bin the moment he'd sent her fleeing from the dining area and that kiss. She raised her hand to her cheek. Her heart was pounding as if he were still standing not an inch from her, heat in his eyes that burned into her soul.

The sputter of the peppers in the pan snapped her attention back and she removed it from the heat, with only a little bee sting from the oil. That was what she got for not paying attention. But as she ran the peeler over the courgettes, adding them to the fresh green salad with pistachios that was a favourite of Javier's, she wondered. What if he *did* have amnesia?

Could she do it? Pretend that all the hurt hadn't happened? The hours, days and even weeks sometimes when he hadn't come home. She'd been alone in a country that wasn't hers, unknowing of the language or people who could become friends. The gifts that he'd left in his wake—expensive, absolutely, exquisite, quite probably—but nothing that she would ever have chosen for herself and most definitely poor compensation for the loss of him.

But when they were together… A flush rose to her cheeks that had nothing to do with the heat of the kitchen. There had been a time when they had been pure intense passion. But Emily had soon discovered that it wasn't enough to hold a marriage together. They had needed more. *She* had needed more.

She finished the salad and plated the Padrón peppers with a sprinkle of sea salt and took them out to the table on the green and white tiled patio. The sun was beginning to drop towards the dark craggy outline of the range across the gorge and in the far distance she could see a sliver of the sea, sparkling like a jewel. And, even though her emotions were all over the place, her soul recognised this as home.

In sickness and in health.

The words gently whispered into her mind and she knew that she would give Javier the help he needed. She just wouldn't, couldn't, give more of herself than that. Not this time.

Javier watched his wife standing on the patio from what had once been his favourite room in the house and was now a child's drawing of scribbled colours that hurt his eyes and his head. Gritting his teeth, he braced himself as he levered himself up, enticed more by the prospect of painkillers than food.

He had half imagined that Emily would have made his most hated meal—some evil concoction called corned beef hash that he'd disliked on principle. Meat should never, *ever* come in a tin. Even just the thought of it turned his stomach. But the scent wafting in from the open doors was mouth-wateringly familiar and he couldn't help but be drawn to the table Emily had prepared.

But it was her he gravitated to. As she stood there, staring into the distance, Emily felt as far from his reach as when she'd been in London. His conscience stirred.

'Are you okay?' he was unable to stop himself from asking.

She turned, a rueful smile on lips that had seduced him, had loved him and then cursed him. 'I was about to ask you the same.'

He nodded, allowing them both to avoid the question.

'Morcilla, salad, Padrón peppers, roast aubergine, Manchego… *Dios*, Emily, this is a feast.'

Taking in the table, he was suddenly famished. He didn't know where to start. As if sensing the sheer force of his hunger, she shook her head, a small smile pulling at the corner of her mouth. 'Just go for it.'

And he did. He filled his plate with portions of everything, each part of the meal a delicious taste. The citrus of the lemon-dressed salad, the sweetness of the quince paste for the creaminess of the semi-hard cheese, the salt of the morcilla and the fleshy aubergine.

'I think you have made every single one of my favourites.'

'Yes,' his wife replied as if it were obvious.

He looked up at her, leaning back in her chair, glass of white wine in hand and something in her eyes he'd thought he'd never see again. It poked at him and he didn't like it. But she must have misread the confusion in his gaze.

'It's what you do when someone is not well.'

'What?' he asked, this time definitely confused.

She frowned at his response. 'You make the person's favourite foods.'

The taste of Manchego and *membrillo* dried on Javier's tongue and he reached for his water. He nodded and looked up to find her watching him. He smiled at her and speared a piece of aubergine, filling his mouth to prevent a retort.

No. That hadn't been what his mother had ever done for him when he'd been unwell.

She'd either refused to accept any sign of illness, or had drowned him in lavish, overwhelming and completely disproportionate concern—aimed at garnering attention for herself rather than her son. The idea of something as simple as making his favourite foods was strange and somewhat painful to consider. It made him feel awkwardly envious and resentful, as if he were on the outside looking in on how *normal* people lived.

'What did your mother make you?' he asked around the dry sand in his throat.

His wife held his gaze. 'Corned beef hash.'

He nearly choked on the mouthful until he saw the humour star-lighting her eyes. He swallowed around his smile and, more out of habit than curiosity, asked, 'How is she?'

She knew what he'd done, changing the conversation to distract her. But she'd felt such a sense of *pain* following the careless comment she'd made about making him his favourite foods it shocked her. In the past, Javier had been so adept at hiding his feelings but this time she felt his confusion, his loss, as if it had been her own. Yet, despite this, Javier looked at her expectantly.

Her mother. Emily felt the familiar tension across her shoulders and looked away from the table, out over the gorge to the sprinkle of early stars dusting the dusk sky. She had gathered herself by the time she looked back to Javier.

'She's much the same. She and Steven are still in Morden and...' she shrugged, not quite sure what else to add '...they're good,' she concluded. Javier's hawklike gaze focused in on the pause like a sign of weakness. The last time she had seen them had been just over six months ago. Before Christmas, because her stepfather liked their annual 'cruise at Christmas'.

The memory scratched at a wound that was only slightly dulled by time and Emily felt foolish for nursing the hurt. She had been sixteen when she had incorrectly assumed she was to join them on their Christmas holiday. She'd never forgotten the look in her mother's eyes as she'd silently begged Emily not to make a fuss, not to say anything. So she hadn't. She'd stayed behind because she was old enough, and had spent the entire festive period alone. And the following year there hadn't been any question of her joining them.

Each year was a fresh hurt over an old ache and she would feel foolish and guilty, because she knew that her mother was happy. She loved Steven, of that there was no doubt. So how could Emily resent her mother finding happiness after all that she'd been through? It had been just her and her mother for the first eleven years of her life and, while her mother had made it magical and wondrous, even as a child Emily hadn't been blind to the hardship and the exhaustion and the financial worry that her mother had tried to hide. So Emily's conscience poked and prodded, reminding her that her mother deserved to be happy.

She felt fingers wrap around hers where it held the stem of the wine glass and jerked at the unexpected contact, sloshing the wine over the edge, and let out a startled laugh. 'Sorry,' she said, reaching for a tea towel to mop up the spill.

'Things are not better between you?' Javier asked, concern clear in his gaze.

'They're fine,' she said again, the bland words dull on her tongue.

'So they haven't let you redecorate? I thought you would have painted over every inch of beige in that house.'

The tease pulled a smile from her, which faded at the memory of how her mother and stepfather had behaved when she and Javier visited to let them know they were married.

'I'm sorry. I'm *still* sorry,' she clarified, 'at their behaviour during that visit.' She shook her head, even now wondering if that had somehow been the beginning of the end of their fantastical romance. 'Steven has the emotional intelligence of an amoeba and the social skills of a toad.'

'But it is such a delightful combination, *mi cielo*,' Javier said, the sarcasm playful and the endearment intimate. 'And, of course, you have met my mother. There is no competition,' he said, the sweep of his free hand clearing any further debate.

Mi cielo.

It whispered into the night, reminding her of a thousand sighs and kisses and touches, warming her body beneath the cool breeze. She pulled her hand from beneath his and *still* the feeling of heat brushed across the back of her neck.

'So, the doctor told me that the last thing you really remember was Gabi's sixteenth birthday?'

The turn in the conversation was sudden and jarring. There was a hint of wariness in the question that hadn't been there since she'd opened the door to him. He resented the intrusion of that unease. For just a moment, he had felt the connection he'd shared with Emily flare to life once again, deeper than just the sense of attraction that was a dull throb across his body. His wife *hurt* and he wanted to take that away. But she wouldn't let him.

The thought took him back to the last months they had shared under this roof. The way she had retreated further and further from him and, no matter how hard he'd worked, tried to provide for her, he'd known—felt—time running out. It had been as if she were slipping through his fingers like sand and nothing he'd done had been able to stop it. For just a second, his lungs seized with the same kind of helpless anguish he'd experienced in those last few months of their marriage. That sense of inadequacy that cut right through to his deepest vulnerability.

Alto.

She was looking at him expectantly, and he shook off the thought. She wanted to know what he remembered, and he would have to be *very* careful about how he answered.

'Yes. The doctor advised me not to ask questions, or force the memories of what has happened since then.'

In fact, Javier's doctor had been just as suspicious as Emily seemed to be, though unwilling to specifically call him on it. His advice had been full of hypotheticals. *'If you can't remember...' 'If you feel that...'* All coming on the heels of a warning.

'I have met your mother, so perhaps I understand a little. But your wife is a different matter, Mr Casas. She looks like she'd fight fire with fire.'

It had been a timely warning and one that he reminded himself to heed.

'Is it as if the party was only yesterday for you?'

'Not quite,' he hedged. 'More as if that's the last thing I can remember. It's clear that time has passed. We look older, and there are some things I know,' he said, making it as ambiguous as possible. 'Yet things don't fit together coherently.'

She watched him steadily.

'But I remember what you were wearing that night,' he said truthfully. The image was as clear to him now as if it *had* been yesterday. She had been stunning in a white jumpsuit with a neck that veed tantalisingly deep. Cuts in the sleeves allowed the material to drape either side of her forearms, looking timeless and elegant. 'How you looked, how the scent rising from your skin hit me here.' He thudded a fist to his chest. 'How it reminded me of the first time we met and how all I wanted to do that night was take you to bed.'

Her pupils flared at his praise, the flush to her cheeks familiar and filling him with an aching want that he knew wouldn't be appeased that night. Once again, her lips parted ever so slightly, and he stopped himself from reaching across the table to plump her bottom lip with the pad of his thumb.

He'd clung to Emily that night, his gaze, his focus expertly blocking out his mother's hysterical attempts to steal her daughter's limelight on her sixteenth birthday. Hysteria that had been blessedly in remission for the three years preceding. But with the breakdown of her third marriage Renata Casas had returned to form.

Heart still pounding from the force of his adamant memory of her that night, Emily felt herself swaying towards her husband. It would be so easy to pretend that the last six years hadn't happened. To indulge in a passion that was still utterly undeniable.

Touch. It wasn't only what she'd missed about him, but it was a significant part. His touch had brought her to life, had shown her what passion could be, that it had colour, texture, taste and scent. That passion was luxurious and powerful and empowering... He had taken her from that drab beige, unhappy world of hers and thrust her into Technicolor. He had magicked her into a real girl—living and breathing and passionate. And then he had abandoned her.

Desperate to hold onto any thread that would keep her sane, she forced her thoughts away from dangerous ground.

'Gabi was worried about you,' she said, unable to forget the way his sister had held so tightly onto her hand, sure that the strength was hers to give to Gabi rather than the other way round.

Javier's penetrating stare threatened to smother her, accusing her of avoiding the shocking sensuality caused by the scattering of his words. For a moment, she wondered whether he would push the issue. He had in the past. He had wielded their passion like a conductor wielded his baton, deft fingers setting a pace and rhythm that could nearly have ruined her, pulling a melody from her soul that she was unable to deny.

But instead he nodded, a darkness shadowing his gaze. 'I worry about her. I believe that she is still living with my mother?'

For a moment she was about to admit that she didn't know. But if he had lost his memory, then he would want to know *why* she didn't know because she would, wouldn't she? A lack of sleep, a fury of adrenaline, a sense of... *something* building on the horizon all added to what promised to be a spectacular headache. She ran her fingers across her forehead, trying to soothe the tension, a gesture Javier didn't miss.

'Yes,' she eventually answered, having gathered that his sister was still living with his mother from the few exchanges she'd overheard in the hospital.

A frown flickered across Javier's brow but he did not share his thoughts. Which was another thing Emily remembered from her time with him. How closed-off he had kept her from his family. At first she had thought that they were not particularly close, but over the months of their marriage Renata had called again and again and every time Javier would go. It was a strange thing—as if it were duty, a weary one. But Emily had been reeling from her own hurt from a mother who barely saw her any more. That, combined with a husband who had spent more time away from her than not, had left her feeling vulnerable and lonely. In fact, this was the longest she remembered Javier spending without looking at his phone.

'What about work? Your businesses...will they be okay?'

She could imagine the panic and fear of his employees and company boards caused by the prospect of his memory loss, temporary or even perhaps lasting. She had lost count of the articles she'd seen over the years about the number of businesses he now owned.

He discarded her question with a sweep of his hand. 'Yes, I've spoken to my assistant. It will be fine. Would you like more wine? I'll get some,' he announced, excusing himself from the table before he saw Emily's reaction.

As if she had been struck, Emily froze—his words turning her to stone.

'It will be fine.'

The Javier Casas of six years ago would never, ever have said such a thing. In fact, the Javier Casas of six years ago would have already spent four hours working, desperate to catch up with his business affairs. So there was absolutely no way that the Javier of six years ago would think for even a second that his business would be fine without him.

The bastard.

He *was* lying. And this time she knew it with such force she practically trembled with rage.

Javier was congratulating himself on how well it was going as he retrieved a bottle of white wine from the fridge. He was tempted to have a glass, but doubted that mixing alcohol with strong painkillers was a good idea. And although he had navigated the tricky waters of his memory loss with Emily well, he knew that he would need all his wits about him. As it was, he was already fighting a tiredness that was shocking in its intensity.

He took the wine back out to the table to find Emily looking out at the gorge rising above the Higuerón River. And he stopped. Struck by a shocking and unwelcome wave of déjà vu, his lungs seized and the knife twisted.

How many times had he imagined her here, at the house in Frigiliana, standing just like that, in his mind's eye? Whether he'd been in Madrid, Barcelona, whether he'd been further afield in Svardia, or Tokyo, or Pakistan, somehow he'd always imagined her here.

Javier had achieved incomparable success in the business world—more than half of which was a closely guarded secret. From the first company he'd owned, given to him by his uncle, who knew Renata Casas would never share the textile empire she considered solely hers, Javier had been driven. Driven to pay his uncle back, to prove that he was worthy of the gift he'd been given. And, with one heart-stopping investment, he'd made enough money to do just that, and more. He had expanded from one business to two, then three and so on. But if his mother had the slightest inkling of how much he was worth…carnage. It would be carnage.

But back then Javier had been driven by the need to prove himself, working like the devil himself, spending every hour he could, just to have something that couldn't be taken away from him. Something that was his…to share with his wife. But she had left him on the very night that he'd planned to tell her of his success. His hand tightened around the bottle of wine.

Javier had meant his vows, determined not to make the same mistakes as his parents. He had wanted a family. A wife, children, the laughter that had so drawn him to Emily from the very first—he'd wanted that sound in his life every day. How had he forgotten that? Looking at the silhouette she made against the night sky, he put the bottle of wine down and made a decision. Enough was enough. It was time for Emily to come home. And if he had to play the amnesia game to make it happen, he would. He would remind them both of how great they'd been together. There had certainly never been a problem with their attraction—the spark of desire had always burned like phosphorus in pure oxygen—molten, bright and white-hot.

He would—

'I think I'm going to head to bed.' His wife's

words cut short and twined with his thoughts and a smile pulled at his lips.

'That would be delightful, *mi amor*.'

A different sort of smile painted Emily's lips and something sharp blinked in her eyes before it was gone.

'I shall see you tomorrow then.'

'We can go together?' he said, leaning in, unable to deny himself the hint of honeysuckle in her perfume. She looked up at him, his gut clenched. How had he forgotten how petite she was? Suddenly his mind was awash with erotic images that stole his mind and his breath. Her hand rose to press against his chest, where she would surely feel the thunder of his heartbeat. He felt claimed by it, until she opened her mouth.

'Javi…' The sing-song tone of her voice was at odds with the sensual web he was caught in. 'You know that the doctor ordered separate beds.'

'I know no such thing!' His outrage was swift and clear.

'Well, *that* was what he told *me*. You'll be okay getting to bed on your own?' Emily asked, knowing that Javier would see it as a challenge.

His response, 'Of course,' was a relief. She really didn't think that she could help him to bed. Not now that she knew he was lying to her. Anger, a hot and wild thing, unravelled in her and drew pinpricks of heat across her skin that hurt.

Emily got to the spare room, readied herself for bed and changed into her nightgown, lying down on a bed in a room that she had once hoped to make a nursery with the man she loved. With a man she had loved. But that man had been taken away from her and the thief was sleeping in the next room. A tear escaped and a line was drawn.

And as Javier Casas planned a seduction for his wife, Emily Casas planned their divorce.

CHAPTER FOUR

JAVIER WOKE UP feeling a sense of serenity he hadn't known in years.

His wife's redecoration efforts hadn't stopped in the lower sections of the house, but here in this room it had been something wondrous. As if Emily couldn't bring herself to make it awful. What had once been simple white walls accentuating the stunning greenery of the gorge through floor-to-ceiling windows was now...magical. There was no other word to describe it, and Javier was not one to use that word lightly.

The room was still sparsely furnished, the simple lines of the large wooden bedframe and the curved arch doorway to the en suite bathroom deeply satisfying. But she had bridged the area where the wall met the window with a thousand plants. Ones with trails, or little balls, some heart-shaped and others like tongues, but the sense of this room—it felt *alive*. As if she'd drawn the outside in and there was no glass, no separation between them and the rich landscape beyond. It softened a space he hadn't realised needed changing.

He threw back the covers and felt fire. A sudden, painfully bright, piercing jabbed into his ribs, catching his lungs in a death grip and tightening already bruised muscles along his side.

Cabrón.

He waited for the tremors to subside, the waves of pain to retreat, and forced his breathing to slow. He hadn't felt this helpless since he was a child and even the thought of it had him gritting his teeth. He forced himself up and, although it was slow going, made it to the bathroom, where he stared down the painkillers he'd left on the counter.

Emily hadn't made any changes that he could see to the room, but that didn't mean he trusted her not to have booby-trapped something. The thought had him expel a laugh that hurt more than he liked. So he reluctantly reached for the pill bottle and dry swallowed a tablet.

The light behind the mirror glowed golden across the unusual paleness of his skin and for the first time since the accident he took in the damage to his body. The bruise across his cheekbone had settled into a yellow-tinged purple which looked far worse than the angry red it had been, even if it was a sign of healing. He winced as he gently prodded the dissolvable stitches used by the plastic surgeon his mother had demanded—but his healthcare had paid for—on the cut on his forehead.

Javier had never been a vain man and he was always amused by how that surprised so many people. Scar or no scar, his only concern was how infuriatingly itchy the area was. Healing, again. He'd been warned. But… Not enough. He'd not been warned enough. Or maybe he just hadn't wanted to listen.

In the next room, Emily was probably sleeping and the thought of it made a mockery of all the times he had delighted in waking her up with kisses that turned into gentle touches, and caresses that turned into sighs of pleasure and the taste of her on his tongue. In mere seconds, Javier was hard and angry.

She had taken that away from them. Years of time they could have been happy. He turned on the tap and splashed ice-cold water across his face, wondering just how long it would take for the painkillers to kick in and just how quickly he could bring his wife to his mercy.

He thought of the flare in her eyes last night, as he'd reminded her of Gabi's sixteenth. He thought of the need building within him and the urge to take advantage of the passion that had been like nothing else he'd ever known from the very first moment he'd seen her.

But he wouldn't.

No. He would never.

But he also thought of the concern and confusion he'd seen in her eyes. She had started to doubt her belief that he was faking, he knew it. And through the course of the evening he'd persuaded her that his memory loss was real. He'd felt it, her softening, melting, the way she had done in the past whenever she'd argued about the money he'd wanted to lavish on her or the gifts he'd bought her to compensate for the hours he'd worked. A slow, inevitable yielding as he'd got his way. A victory of sorts—one that was only marginally less sweet than what it would feel like to have her back by his side and in his bed.

Emily stared at the steam unfurling from the second espresso she'd made since finally giving up on sleep and trying to stop the circular thoughts from spinning around her head. Javier was punishing her, she was sure of it. Punishing her for leaving him, even if she hadn't wanted to. Even if she hadn't intended to. Because really she'd thought he'd come for her when he realised she'd gone. Thought that he'd rush to her side with apologies and promises that their marriage would be like it had been at the very beginning. But he hadn't. Not once had he reached out to her.

It's not as if you reached out to him.

No, she thought, she hadn't—*couldn't*—bring herself to call him. Because it would have hurt too much to beg, to plead with him to see her, to love her. Emily's heart throbbed. *That* was why she'd needed him to come for her. Why she'd needed him to make the first move. So she would know that it hadn't been a mistake. That they hadn't just been caught up in the passion of it all. That there was something real binding them together. That it hadn't just been *her* in this marriage alone.

She heard the slap of his bare feet on the stone steps leading down from the first floor, gathering herself in a panic. Javier clearly thought she believed his act. But he had forgotten how well she knew him. Nothing would keep him from his precious businesses. Not his sickbed and certainly not fake amnesia! So, no. He had underestimated her and this time she would have him at her feet, begging for forgiveness.

The steps, slow and hesitant, an unusual amount of time between them, poked and prodded at her conscience, but the gleam in his eye last night as he had teased her with the almost desperate sensuality between them cast her will in iron.

A perfect smile was on her lips as Javier rounded the corner and an almost imperceptible pause stuttered his steps, before they doubled in speed as he came down the remaining steps.

'Good morning, *mi amore*,' he said, reaching her, only a slight wariness in his gaze as if he were trying to predict what she might do next.

The fire that had kept her up all night fizzed and sparked, driving her towards an impulsiveness that she was unaccustomed to. He had thought to subdue her with desire and it was maddening. But she wasn't the only one who had been enslaved by their passion.

If he was surprised by the way she stood up from her chair, pressed herself against his body, wound her hands around his neck and pulled him into a kiss that could have scorched all thought from both parties, then he didn't show it. As if it were the most natural thing in the world, his arm swept around her waist and pulled her against him as Emily's intention only to use his own tactics against him spun wildly out of control.

The moment his tongue laved her bottom lip she was helpless to refuse him. She barely had a moment to prepare for how he took ruthless possession of her mouth in a way that made her pulse pound in her heart and between her legs. The growl that purred from his throat lifted the hairs on the back of her neck as his hand gripped the hair above her nape, angling her firmly back to allow him deeper, to allow him more of her and—helpless and wanton—she let him.

Anger and desire melded as she wrestled for control, biting down not so gently on his lip. His eyes sprung open and *burned.* For a frantic second she teetered on the brink of a precipice, wishing she hadn't been so impulsive... But then he walked them back against the dining room wall, pressing her, crowding her, tormenting her as his hands ravished her body, palming breasts with nipples hardened to peaks, fisting the flesh of her backside in a way that would be worth every ache.

This, she thought. *This* was what she dreamed of at night when her lust-addled mind taunted her with erotic pictures from before he had begun to work all hours, before the doubt and worry had crept in. Before she questioned if she had given up everything for a man who was no longer there.

Her head fell back and she felt feasted upon. He drew her against the rock-hard length of his need and she gasped, biting her lip to prevent the plea on her tongue. Words that would beg and bribe lodged in her throat as her heart ached and wanted and angered all at once.

He sneaked deft fingers behind her knee and drew her leg up to hook over his hip, gently pressing his way deeper against the throbbing ache that was almost painful in its intensity. She was helpless to stop herself from pressing back, from shifting in a way that caressed and eased and tormented her own arousal whilst teasing and hardening Javier's.

His eyes flared open, pinning her with an incomprehensible gaze that whispered only one word to her: *more*. She felt her orgasm begin to build beneath his watchful gaze, urged on by the voyeuristic enjoyment he found in her pleasure. Muscles tightened on an emptiness deep within, but outside everything burned, wanted, needed. More. She wanted more. Because she knew how good he felt deep within her. Knew what it was to be possessed by this man. To be owned.

As if a bucket of ice-cold water had slapped over her, she tensed. A scream stopped in her throat. No. She could not be owned by him. Not again. She'd not survive it.

'What?' Javier whispered, alarmed by the sudden change in Emily. His hands went to cup her face but she wriggled from them.

'Sorry, I've...' and she sneaked beneath his arm, escaping the circle of his embrace.

His breath straining in aching lungs, he stared at her, trying to ignore the sliver of hurt that cut more deeply than any wound from the accident. 'Are you okay?'

'Of course,' she insisted, spinning back round to face him, a smile on her lips as fake as the five-foot ceramic parrot in the sitting room. Lips that had teased him to the point of near orgasm only seconds earlier. *Cristo*, he'd not been this out of control since their first time together.

'I just forgot that I have to go out.'

'Out?'

Javier detested intensely that he was sounding like an idiot, reduced to monosyllabic questions. But it was taking him a worryingly long time to get his usually hair-triggered brain out of the lust-fuelled fantasy of taking his wife on the table once again.

'Yes, out,' she said, her eyes wide, blush riding high on her cheeks, hair in disarray from where he had gripped and—

She reached blindly for her keys.

'What are you going out for?' he asked, amazed that the words formed some semblance of order.

'Food.'

'But we have—'

She spun away from him and was out through the front door before he could finish.

'—food,' he said to an empty house.

He swallowed, an act he both felt and heard. The sound of the door closing behind her had snapped a thread on the rope tying his emotions down and he felt something crawling, clawing, trying to get out. Shoving it down with more force than usual, he stalked into the kitchen and made himself a coffee.

He needed something to cover the taste of lust on his tongue. He rearranged his trousers to relieve the pressure against the wildfire ache Emily had drawn from him as if she were a magician pulling his desire like silk scarves from her pocket. The moment she had pressed her lips against his he'd been lost, only returning to his sense of self when she had fled his embrace.

He took his coffee out to the patio, wondering at the effect she had on him, when his phone buzzed in his pocket.

How is OP AM coming along?

He typed back to Santiago.

OP AM??

Operation Amnesia. I'm prepared to offer for the movie rights.

Javier stared at his phone, trying to work out if his oldest friend was joking. Clearly he had taken too long because the next message came through before he could reply.

Is Emily back?

Santi had been there the night he'd first met Emily. They had, in fact, been at the bar so that Santi could finally work up the courage to ask out Mariana—which had taken perhaps a little too much whisky, but had been successful nonetheless. Santi had been insufferably in love then and had been more than a little smug in the intervening years with his exceedingly happy marriage—to the point of trying to meddle in his own.

They had almost come to blows when Javier wouldn't go after Emily. It was the first—and only—real argument they'd ever had. But even his closest friend couldn't understand the devastating betrayal of Emily's sudden, silent departure from his life. How it had made old wounds run with fresh blood. No. Javier could never have gone after her.

Santi hadn't understood that, but it didn't

stop him from being closer to him than a brother, one of the best filmmakers in the world, *and* the reason that Javier had made his first million. The nail-biting seven months Javier had to wait to find out whether his investment in Santiago's first film would pay off had been the most stressful of his life. He had been so unsure of success that he'd worked nineteen-hour days to cover the financial gap in his business in case it didn't pay off—unwilling to tell his uncle what he had done, knowing Gael wouldn't understand, and knowing that he could never have admitted to Emily that he had taken such a risk.

But Javier had known it would work. And it had. Spectacularly. From there on out, Javier became one of Santiago's main investors—the revenue from the film industry a small fortune in its own right. And in Javier's hands money turned into property and investments and companies, ranging from import to technology, communications and media. *Infierno*, he doubted even he could say the names of all the companies he part owned or funded.

He had amassed a fortune that had brought him to the attention of the highest—and sometimes most secretive—echelons of society and he had determined to do as much good as he could with his wealth.

But somehow that didn't matter a damn when Santi had asked, *Is Emily back?* His fist tightened around the phone as he jabbed out his reply.

Not yet. But she will be.

Emily's calves were hurting after stalking the upward winding cobbled streets of Frigiliana, but it was a good hurt. A physical one. It somehow soothed the emotional hurt she'd felt before fleeing their home. She had over-reacted, she realised now. Not to Javier, not to the situation. *That*, she felt justified in. But she was embarrassed by how quickly her plan had backfired. Clearly she couldn't be trusted anywhere near Javier's lips, or hands...or body for that matter.

Even now the thought of it made her pulse leap, her skin flush and filled her with that indescribable yearning that flared low in her body. She looked up in time to dodge a tourist couple taking photographs in front of the spectacular bougainvillea pouring down the white walls of the town like a fountain.

She'd had no particular destination in mind when she'd left, but now her feet traced paths she'd taken with Javier when they had first come to Frigiliana, hand in hand, or tucked under the wide protection of his shoulders. The way his hand would trace the hemline of her skirt, caressing her thigh secretively and sending her wild. The way he would stop and talk to almost every shop owner or business owner, a question and an interest in everyone and everything. And she hadn't minded. She'd just soaked it all up.

Six years ago she'd unfurled beneath the sun and Javier's heated touch. She'd felt herself becoming the woman she was always supposed to be. Colourful, bright, happy. It had been so different from the beige, bored silence of the home she had shared with her mother and Steven. And she'd found herself angry with her mother all over again. Not for herself but for what her mother had lost. Because she too had once lived in the bright colours of summer. When Emily was young, her mother had been bright and bold. She had laughed and loved and lavished her attention on her daughter. But Steven had stolen that light, dimmed it. After they married it was as if her mother laughed to fill a silence, not because there had been joy. And the betrayal that Emily had felt…it had devastated her and confused her, scratched at her heart, making her feel guilty, angry, hurt and selfish.

She was suddenly the spoiled only child who

didn't want to share her mother. But it wasn't that. Not at all. It was just that the woman who married Steven wasn't the same woman who had been her mother. And it had felt like the slowest loss played out in front of her each night as, hour by hour, her mother changed into someone who revolved only around her husband, as if she were sacrificing slices of herself over and over again until there was nothing left of the mother that Emily had once known.

Emily went to brush away the sudden trail of ice on her cheek, only to realise that a tear had fallen. She shook off the memories of the past and looked around at the town that had changed only a little in the last six years. Some of the shops were different, but there was still the silver jewellery shop on the first fork in the path, the bakery that would sell out before nine in the morning, the tourist shops with racks of sunglasses and hats for the unprepared. But it was the patterned cobbles that she loved the most, the little courtyards tucked off the main walkways behind peeling iron gates, and the Hand of Fatima door knockers standing out against painted doors.

As she continued down the cobbled street she saw a shop she didn't remember. Space-Whale's doorway was framed by large green palms and snake plants, enticing Emily into the welcoming shade and away from the intense heat of the mid-morning. Inside she found a cornucopia of delights. Stunning prints and photographs, hypnotic incense and candles, jewellery, books, stationery. Not knowing where to look first, she found herself drawn to the scents and couldn't resist picking up a small bottle of perfume that was rich and sensual and felt as if it belonged to the wife of Javier Casas more than herself in that moment. Without questioning it, she paid for the perfume and took the shop's card—instinctively knowing that she would come back, either for herself or for her clients.

On her way out, she noticed a board pinned with announcements and local adverts. A picture of the most hideous cat she'd ever seen had caught the attention of several passers-by and a lot of laughter. As she drew closer, she read the announcement.

Ready for rehoming.
Be warned, this cat is possessed.

Emily hid a laugh behind her hand, but couldn't resist reading on. It warned of an evil cat that hissed, snapped, bit and clawed. It had been placed with seven different homes now and not one had lasted more than two days. Notoriously violent with men, the notice concluded with the challenge of rehoming...*if you dare*.

Eyes narrowed, smile pulling at the corner of her lips, Emily began to plan.

Two hours later Emily was unloading bags, boxes, trays, cases and more bags from the taxi she'd had to get to drive her home. She'd had to pay the driver extra because of her precious cargo, so she was surprised that he got out to help her unload, until she realised it was so he could get rid of them as quickly as possible.

Deciding it was safe to leave the bags outside while she unlocked the door, that giddy thrill of doing something wicked fizzed in her bloodstream again. Meeting Javier's nefariousness with her own was becoming an addictive game. One she warned herself against enjoying too much because, for the first time in a very long time, she was *enjoying* herself. Pitting her intelligence against Javier's was exciting.

She opened the front door and hooked it back against the wall and—

Gasped.

Javier was on the floor with his hand pressed against his head. She rushed over to him, horror flooding her veins and a sob stuck in her throat.

'Javi! Are you okay? What happened?' She

cursed as she reached him, her hands shaking and her whole body trembling.

His unfocused eyes found hers and his expression changed to one of concern. He reached out and caught her wrists to steady her, his eyes snagging on the tears of shock filling her vision. 'Emily, what's wrong?'

Infuriated, she reared back. 'Javi! You are on the floor, what is wrong with *you*?'

He winced and gently rolled his head from side to side until he stared at the door, confusion once again filling his gaze.

'Emily. What is *that*?'

CHAPTER FIVE

HE WAS GOING to take great satisfaction in destroying that ceramic parrot. After he found out what the hell it was that was hissing at him from inside a small cage.

Mierda, his head hurt. Coming through from the patio, he'd had his phone in one hand, coffee in the other when he'd startled at the sight of the big white bird. Not that he would admit it to any living soul, but he'd jumped, spilling the coffee, and then—humiliatingly—had slipped on it and fallen. With his hands full and his stomach muscles already bruised, his body had reacted more slowly than usual and he'd landed on the floor, winded and aching.

He looked up at Emily, her expression unsure and guilt painting slashes of red over her lush cheekbones. She flicked her gaze between him and the cage and bit her lip.

'It's…it's…your…erm… It's our…'

Her eyes grew wider each time she tried

to explain, the words seeming to bottleneck in her throat, and curiosity and pain were the only things that stopped him from laughing out loud.

Oh, God, what fresh hell was this?

He peered at the crystalline eyes glaring daggers at him from the small crate and the clawed paw that looked alarmingly threatening.

'We have a cat?' he asked, knowing full well they didn't.

Emily nodded quickly, blonde hair quivering around her like a shimmering halo.

'She's been at the cattery. While you were...' Her hand slipped from where he still held it, and gestured in circles—and a memory surfaced of her doing exactly the same thing when she had lied about something silly years before. One thing was for sure. His wife should never play poker.

But, he realised as he gently rested his head back down against the floor, his wife apparently *didn't* believe his amnesia and had found a new way to torment him. The cat—without a shadow of a doubt—was one of the ugliest things he'd ever seen.

He wanted to ask where the cat's fur was, but instead he asked, 'Her name?', while his mind recalibrated this new information about his devious wife.

Emily paused for a second, flicking the cat a glance and only releasing the pin of teeth on her lip to answer, 'Diabla.'

And this time he *did* laugh. *She devil*. It seemed appropriate.

Emily had barely got over her shock when it morphed into anger again. But she refused to give him the satisfaction of knowing how worried she had been. The stubborn, mule-headed, infuriating man deserved every single thing coming to him.

When she'd first seen him lying on the floor, her heart had stopped. Actually stopped. Only to start again with a whoosh that sent electric sparks shooting around her body, tingling her fingertips, pricking her heart and trembling her hands.

It was the second time he'd done this to her and it was too much, she'd decided angrily as she'd let Diabla out of the cage. The animal had burst from her confines, pausing only to hiss at Javier before rushing off at an alarming speed. To Emily's surprise, Javier had only laughed even harder.

She'd gone to the freezer, grabbed a bag of peas, retrieved his painkillers and stood over him as—still on the floor—he'd swallowed down two tablets. After that she had gone to her room, shut the door and ignored his attempts to speak to her.

Opening her laptop, she spent an hour fielding emails and assigning workloads to her staff, silently promising them all a pay rise when this was done. She'd never been away from her work or staff this long since she'd started the company and it tore at her to be away from it now.

She remembered Javier's swift dismissal that his businesses would be 'fine'. Well, she was glad *his* interests were fine. They couldn't all have a million and one assistants to cover their vast empires, she thought angrily. And then regretted her thoughts. That was uncharitable and mean. He had always worked hard, despite the money he had been born into. Javier was nothing like the rich men she knew from London: entitled, lazy, loud and bordering on brutish. No, Javier's work ethic had been inspiring, until it had become almost obsessive, until it had taken him away from her for days on end.

At some point Javier left some lunch outside the room, which she'd retrieved and absentmindedly eaten as she'd scanned the plans for the San Antonio project. The mood boards were her starting point, gathering any imagery that was associated with the client and the location. Because she had to bring it *all* together. The client wanted what they wanted, but if it didn't fit the space, if it worked *against* the location, then whatever she created would stick out like a sore thumb. It might, on the surface, be fine, but beneath it would be simmering discontent. So she threw herself into colours and moods and textures and, before she knew it, four hours had passed and her back ached.

But it had been worth it because Emily had finally got that feeling—the thrill of finding *the thing*. And suddenly everything slotted together: the patterns she wanted to use, the light fittings and the wall panels, the textures for some of the furnishings, even the style of crockery, all coming from a paint colour called Mountain Dawn.

It had caught her eye because she'd seen exactly that same rich buttery yellow that morning, creeping over the hill line above the gorge. It was a yellow that fitted against a dusky blue and a rich blush, a deep cobalt and a startlingly clean white. And the range of colours were perfect for San Antonio and her client. And now she was happy and eager to press on…but not until she'd seen where the next two weeks would take her.

Changing into a bikini she'd left behind

the last time she was here, she hoped that the pool's cool water might soothe the anxiety skittering beneath her skin. She wrapped a robe around her and slipped quietly down the stairs, wanting to make it to the pool without alerting Javier. She just wasn't ready to confront him at the moment. She was bruised by his lies, and scared by her concern for him, a man she was seriously considering divorcing.

Because, really, what kind of relationship was this? She had wants and needs that couldn't be put on hold for another six years—a home, family, children… People she wanted to love and be loved by. What had started as a yearning a few years ago was becoming stronger and harder to ignore. She owed it to herself to try for more. She deserved more than this strange limbo she had been in since she'd left.

She snuck into the kitchen to retrieve the cat food she'd bought for Diabla. Emily shook the dry biscuits so the cat would know that food was there, her heart jumping a little as she caught sight of the clear blue gaze peeking around the door frame. She poured a large helping into a bowl and placed it on the little balcony, wondering why the cattery had given her such a bad reputation. Deciding that Diabla was simply misunderstood, while vainly hoping that she might scratch just a little at Javier,

Emily made her way outside, where the early evening sun still had enough heat to warm the skin.

She sat at the pool's edge and took in the natural quiet that was particular to Frigiliana. Birds twittered, leaves rustled, a goat bleated somewhere in the distance, and it was the most restful kind of quiet she'd heard in years. She inhaled the scent of lemons from the fruit trees below and wondered if she had been wrong to leave this place.

Strange that it had all been because of a dress. Full of sequins and sparkle and Javier's expectation, it had been both beautiful and terrible when she'd seen it on the bed next to an invitation to a film premiere three days later. Beautiful because it was truly gorgeous, and terrible because the gift had come the very same evening he had left her waiting on a private runway for three hours, having completely forgotten that he'd agreed to come to her friend's party.

That night she'd realised that she'd never be able to go to Santi's film premiere, never make it through the night without breaking down. Part of her had worried that all the months of loneliness and desperate need to be loved would come pouring out in humiliating desperation, but the larger part—the far greater fear—was that, even if she did, it wouldn't matter. Because, deep down, she worried that she had tied herself for the rest of her life to a man who would never love her back.

She brushed a tear from her cheek and kicked her legs in the water. Heart heavy and thoughts swirling, she took a deep breath, let herself fall.

Javier had worried the entire time his wife had locked herself in her room, hating the way that it made him feel on the outside looking in. *Cristo,* it was worse than when she'd been in London.

He knew he'd scared her. For a moment, he'd scared himself. He rolled the shoulder that had a new ache he could add to his collection. He'd not had an accident or hurt himself since…he rubbed at the scar on his collarbone…since he'd learned not to, he thought darkly.

At age seven, he'd walked around with a broken collarbone for nearly twenty-four hours until his teacher had noticed something wrong and sent him to hospital. He'd fallen the day before on his bicycle, but his mother had told him he was trying to ruin her day, trying to take the attention away from her. She'd demanded to know why she had been sent such ungrateful, mean children: Gabi who cried all the time and Javi who just took and took and took. She'd called him a succubus and though he hadn't known the word, he'd understood what his mother had meant.

Things might have been different if it had happened on one of her 'good' days. Renata would have rushed him to hospital, primarily so that she could bathe in the lavish praise of being the perfect mother she sometimes liked to be seen as. But it hadn't been a good day. Renata had just split with her second husband and she was always especially difficult when that happened. But he'd still asked her.

Please, Mamá, it hurts.

The memory of it brought a visceral nausea that threatened to overwhelm him, even now. He'd never told anyone what it had been like growing up with his mother. Santi had guessed enough but even he didn't know the truth of how terrifying it was not to know what mood she would be in. Obsessively loving could flip to vicious jealousy in the blink of an eye. Most of her erratic behaviour had been excused by her family as *dramatic*, but Javier had always suspected that his uncle knew.

In his father's absence, his mother's brother, Gael, had taken Javier under his wing and instructed him in the wider family business. Javier had worked in some capacity in every one of his uncle's businesses since he was fourteen years old, before being entrusted with a small delivery service company on his eighteenth birthday.

Gael's gift had been more than Javier had ever expected, because his mother wouldn't willingly relinquish control of the textile empire she had inherited from her father. He remembered the time he'd had the temerity to ask her if one day he might run it, like she did. Renata had looked him dead in the eye and, with more seriousness than he'd ever seen from her, replied, *'Never.'*

No. She would never relinquish control of that company. Anything Javier had achieved was because of his uncle. But the difficulty there was the anger. An anger he tried to bury against the man who had allowed his mother to get away with what she did. But it was because of that anger that he'd impetuously used money from the start-up property business to invest in Santi's first film.

The complex emotions seethed through his veins, making him feel close to an edge he didn't want to approach. Being with Emily was forcing him to feel things that he had managed well enough to leave alone for the last six years. And now he was beginning to wonder if it hadn't been stubborn pride keeping him from her, but that it had been easier. His conscience stirred painfully in his chest. Because he'd known that things hadn't been okay between them. Each time he'd come home it was as if another shard had been chipped away and all he'd felt was that he was failing. Letting everyone down—Emily, Gael…he was failing.

'You're just like your father. A coward. A failure.'

He pounded the wall with the side of his fist. No. He was nothing like his father. He wasn't a failure and he didn't walk away. He would fix this with Emily. She would return to his side and they would be happy, dammit.

Because he knew she cared. He'd seen it in her eyes when she'd found him moments after he'd fallen. He'd felt it on his tongue in the taste of her, in the way she'd gripped his shirt and pulled him against her in the kiss that morning. He'd counted it in the pulse rate he'd felt when he'd grasped her wrist. He *knew* it.

He took the steps two at a time down to the lower level and the swimming pool. He could feel it in him, the anger, the argument, the words that they'd never said, the disagreements they'd never had. Oh, they'd had passion in spades but in their last few months together she had taken slow backwards steps away from him and she'd fallen through his fingers like sand. But not this time.

Rounding the corner, he burst out onto the patio to find it…empty.

He frowned, looking around, and couldn't see Emily anywhere. He knew she was out here—he'd seen her from the window.

There was a flash of white at the bottom of the pool—the swimming costume he'd talked Emily into buying six years ago. He'd made her promise to wear it at least three times a week, swimming pool or no, just so he could peel it from her delectable skin.

He looked closer, seeing Emily at the bottom of the deep end of the pool—hair floating around her like golden silk, eyes closed and hauntingly still. He waited for her to surface, something disconcerting needling in his chest. His breath started to become short as he imagined how her lungs must be feeling and still she didn't surface. Alarm quickly replaced anger, a fist to his gut, and his mind skipped over the thought that this was what she'd felt for him after his accident. Maybe even that morning.

Alarm turned to panic and—

Basta ya!

He launched himself into the pool.

Something wrapped firmly around her arms and Emily screamed in shock, water rushing into her mouth the moment it opened. She was dragged up out of the water coughing and spluttering, looking up to find herself staring at a very wet, very close Javier.

Heart pounding and angry from the fright, she slapped at his arm.

He shook her, not to hurt and it didn't hurt, but she felt it—his frustration, his fear, mixing with hers—and she slapped him again.

'What was that for?' he demanded.

'You deserved it!' she bit back.

'Probably. But why?'

Because you're lying to me. Because I've left everything in London for you—again. *Because you make me want you when I* don't *want to*, her inner voice screamed silently.

He shook his head, perhaps realising she couldn't answer his question. Not with this game they were playing.

'What were you doing down there?'

'Breathing,' she snapped sarcastically.

She saw the flex of his jaw, one of the only tells Javier Casas had, and reflexively she swallowed.

All the emotions, the drama and the worry of the last few days, the memories of a husband who hadn't even cared enough about the one thing, *one thing*, that had been so important to her… The ache spread out across her chest and crawled up her throat, her heart hurt all over again, bruised and raw, it thudded under the tide of memories washing again and again over her soul.

'*Mi vida,*' Javier said, sweeping a damp twist of hair from her cheek. 'What's wrong? Please tell me,' he begged.

But here? Now? Javier had encircled her with his arms, that legendary focus and determination all on her, the concern she felt press against her in waves. This was the man she had first met; this was the man who wanted to know her secrets and share them, her desires and make them happen, her hurts and make them better. This was the man she had fallen in love with and she so desperately wanted to pretend. Pretend that he *did* have amnesia.

Pretend that he hadn't lied to her and upended her life for his own selfish reasons. Pretend that the last six years hadn't happened. Pretend that it would be the most natural thing in the world for her to make love to the husband she had given her heart and soul to one Spanish summer's eve. She didn't want to worry about what would happen tomorrow or the next day any more. She wanted the here and now. She wanted her husband.

His hand cupped her cheek, and he was looking at her as if trying to unravel some great mystery she wasn't anywhere near ready for him to see. The white linen shirt he wore had turned see-through, clinging to his skin, and his dark trousers abraded her legs beneath the water. They were both breathing hard with the force of staying afloat in the deep end and, in unspoken agreement, Javier swam them back towards the shallow end, keeping her within the circle of his embrace.

He powered them easily through the water, creating a delicious slip and slide between their bodies, until she felt the gentle curve of the edge of the pool at her back. Encased in his arms, she didn't feel trapped but protected, sheltered, hidden… And here, as dusk was falling, in a pool hidden from the sight of passers-by either on the road or on the gorge, she felt that anything could happen. It whispered like a delicious taunt in her mind and soul until she wanted not just anything, but *everything*.

Intensity zipped from his gaze to her body, she felt it like a carnal stroke over her breasts and beneath the waterline. Javier braced one hand against the stone and held her with the other, even though she could now stand. His fingers burned the flesh at her side through the water and shivers racked her body.

'Are you cold, *querida*?'

She bit her lip and shook her head, her eyes

fastened on his, so that she caught the way his gaze flickered between her lips and her eyes. The way his nostrils flared on a swift inhale and his pupils burst wide, the molten depths promising heat and hardness—all concealment ripped away from his intense gaze showing her a world of want she was so tired of fighting. She wanted, she needed, so Emily closed her eyes and surrendered.

'Kiss me,' she pleaded, no longer caring that she was begging. He had always done this to her. He had always made her feel like this, *want* this. With complete and utter submission.

Javier Casas, the man who the press had dubbed as 'having it all', had never wanted anything more in his entire life. His wife was in his arms, asking him to love her. But he couldn't. Because he was lying to her. That she knew it didn't make a bit of difference. His conscience wrestled with the sheer force of his need for her, the request on her lips an invitation to the sweetest of sins.

'*Please.*'

The word escaped lips he'd kissed a thousand times and it hadn't been anywhere near enough. Memories of the way she would laugh beneath his mouth, the giggle he could bring forth with the lightest of touches in the most specific of places, the sigh when he slipped his hand between her legs, the moan that built with her orgasm, the sound of his name on her tongue as she came, it built until the wall of his desire for her loomed so large it blocked out all reason.

If he'd been worried that she'd be startled by the passion with which he claimed her lips, he was so very wrong. Emily was *inflamed* by it. Her mouth opened to his before he even closed the distance between them. Where he would have held her still, she came alive beneath his touch, raising onto tiptoes, twining her arms around his neck, pressing into his chest, making the blood roar her name in his veins. The taste of her was like manna from heaven and he hadn't realised just how lost he had been until Emily found him in that moment. His heart beat so profoundly that for the wildest second he thought to press a hand against his chest to hold it in place.

Encouraged by the small needy groans she made at the back of her throat—the ones he'd used to learn every single one of her favourite places to be touched and teased—he pulled her against the hard ridge of his arousal, satisfied by the little whimper that tangled in their kiss.

With his nose, he nudged her head back so that he could take tiny nips along her neck and shoulder, then chased the ripple of goosebumps with his tongue across her skin. He hooked the strap of the bikini top with his forefinger, sliding it down her shoulder, smiling to himself. If she'd known how much it had cost, she never would have worn the obscenely expensive item of swimwear. But he'd kept the cost from her because he'd known how good it would be to peel it from her skin.

'The moment I saw this,' he said, his finger releasing the strap and following the curve of the top, '*this* was what I imagined doing, over and over and over again.' He pulled down the cup covering her breast and took it into his mouth, relishing the way she leaned back, pressing her chest forward, wanting, needing more. Cupping her breast, his thumb teasing the taut nipple, he pressed open mouth kisses and went to the other, unable to resist the pull of wanting to have it in his mouth.

Her legs wrapped around his hips and brought his arousal deliciously against her core.

'When you wore this,' he said, between teasing her to distraction with his tongue, 'to Santi and Mariana's engagement party, I nearly had a heart attack,' he went on, smiling at the memory. 'You are never to wear this in public, *mi amore*. I told you that when I gave it to you.'

'Santi and Mariana's engagement party?' Emily asked, pulling back from his embrace and staring at him with startlingly dull eyes.

'Yes? You remember.'

She shook her head and slipped from his arms, bracing her hands against the pool edge and levering herself backwards out of the pool. 'I do,' she said as she reached for her robe. 'But you shouldn't.'

He watched her walk away—brain completely blank—until arousal dissipated and he realised what had happened. He cursed, striking out, sending a wave of water that covered half the patio. Santi and Mariana's engagement party had been only weeks before she'd left him and long after Gabi's sixteenth birthday.

The game was up. There was no more pretending.

He glared at the reflection of himself in the window, frustration and fury rippling out across the water in the pool. It was a good thing, he told himself. Because now? Now *nothing* would stop him from getting her back by his side.

CHAPTER SIX

EMILY PRAYED HE wouldn't come after her. That he'd just let her be—let her recover from the pool. Water dripped down her back from the ropes it had made of her hair. She was trembling with cold now, making a mockery of the intense desire that had shivered across her body before.

'Kiss me.'

She had begged. Shame coursed through her. The man who had left her alone, who had shown a selfishness that had cut so very deep, and she had *begged.* She would have pleaded for more if his words hadn't crashed through the fragile shell-world they'd created from his lies. She would have taken everything he had offered and given more of herself than she would ever have wanted. Her fingers rose to her lips, swollen from kisses that would have only had one logical conclusion: sex. He had kissed her with utter and complete possession, he always had. She shook her head at her own weakness. The fact that she couldn't trust herself around him was humiliating.

'Emily!'

His angry shout echoed around the stone-walled house and she wanted to run. Not because she was afraid of him, but because she didn't know what would happen now that the lies were broken in pieces on the floor. For six years, they had avoided this. Avoided why she had left...why their marriage was broken.

Oh, God.

She wasn't ready for this, not dressed in a bikini she was holding together, soaking wet, and still trembling with desire for him. She ran up the stairs just as she heard him come in from the pool, and slammed the spare bedroom door behind her. Grabbing the cover from the bed, she wrapped it around herself, trying to stop her legs from shaking.

'Emily,' he growled through the door.

'Don't you dare get angry with me,' she yelled back.

'What?'

'You're the one who faked having amnesia!'

'And you're the one who filled our home with tat,' he accused from the other side of the door. 'There is *no* excuse for that ceramic parrot.'

She could almost see the angry slash of his hand as if the door had been invisible.

'Having a husband who lies about a medical condition *is* the excuse!'

'Open the door, Emily.'

'No.'

'I will *not* have this conversation with you through a door!' She could tell he was angry, his accent had thickened and, although she would never be afraid of him, she wasn't quite sure what he would do.

'I... I don't want to see you right now.'

'No? Like you didn't want to see me six years ago when you left me waiting on a red carpet?' he demanded.

'Yes. Pretty much,' she replied glibly.

'Stand back,' he growled.

'What? No, I—'

The moment she heard the wood splinter, she leapt back away from the door. She hadn't been that close to it, but the shock of it startled her. Wood snapped as another bang cracked it from the hinges.

'Javi! What are you doing?' she cried. The door fell into the room, half swinging on the last remaining hinge as Javier, barefooted, white shirt and trousers still plastered to his skin, shoulders heaving, looked ready to explode.

'I am making sure, *wife*, that I can see you when you tell me why you left me. So that when you finally explain why you walked away from me without warning or explanation you can't hide this time.'

'Me?' Emily demanded, fury rising like a phoenix in her soul. 'You're accusing *me* of hiding?' she asked, closing the distance between them, mindless of the destruction at the side of the room. 'Javier Casas, you left me long before I even thought about leaving you.'

Shock blew his pupils wide and, rather than another angry outburst, Javier went completely and unnaturally still. It created a vacuum that pulled at her, that sucked air and breath and emotions towards the vortex that was *him*. She nearly stumbled towards him but he took a step back, stopping her in her tracks.

'How can you say that?' he accused, hurt mixing with anger and a palpable sense of injustice.

'Because it's true!' she insisted.

He shook his head, raising his hand to stop her, and then let it drop before he turned away.

'Wait, now *you* don't want to talk?' she demanded, stepping over a piece of broken door frame. 'You literally kick the door down and you're walking away?'

'I do not wish to say something I will regret.'

'I think it's a little late for that, don't you?' she hurled at his retreating back.

Inside, Javier was shaking with impotent fury. That he'd kicked the door off its hinges was terrible enough. But he'd been so mad, so infuriated that she would run from him again. Leave him with all these *feelings* and nowhere or way to get rid of them.

He clenched his jaw, forcing stillness through his body. This kind of hysterical behaviour, it was too much like his mother. A shiver of self-disgust tripped down his spine and turned his stomach. He had more control than this, he needed to have more control than this.

He stalked into the master bedroom, forcing the buttons of his shirt through the water tightened holes, sorely tempted to rip apart the fabric. Instead he yoked his feelings in time to hear Emily's footsteps enter the room that he'd woken in that morning with such a sense of peace.

He peeled the soaking wet shirt from his shoulders and it hit the floor with a soggy slap.

'We *do* need to talk.' Her voice from behind him was low, a whisper almost, resonating with an emotion that was so close to the wrong kind of surrender it turned his stomach.

He clenched his jaw to stop the denial roar from his throat. Because he knew she was right. Unable to turn until he had better control of himself, he nodded once decisively. It was enough.

'I will meet you downstairs once I have changed.'

His hands went to the button of the trousers that clung claustrophobically to the skin on his legs. Too tight. Everything was too tight.

'Javier—'

'Once I have changed,' he growled, turning to pin her with a stare that allowed no argument.

But he wished he hadn't turned. Because the insecurity in her vivid blue gaze, the way she held herself, a foot tucked behind an ankle, as if making herself as small as possible... A knife cut into his lungs. He had never wanted to see that in his wife: uncertainty, doubt. *He* had done that. He had made her feel those things. And more, his conscience taunted him.

You left me long before I even thought about leaving you.

He wanted to grip his head and make the words stop, but he wouldn't. Because he needed to hear them. He needed to know what had happened if he was going to save his marriage. If he was going to be better than his father. No. Unlike the man who had given him life, who had walked away in shame after failing his family, Javier was going to *fight*—and, no matter how Emily felt about it, she *was* his family.

Emily shifted in the doorway, yanking his attention back to her.

'Put on some dry clothes, or you'll catch a cold,' he commanded before turning to the en suite bathroom and closing the door behind him. But no amount of separation would remove the imprint of her seared into his mind. She had wrapped a throw around her shoulders, but it did nothing to disguise the way that water had clung to her thighs in droplets he wanted to lick from her skin. His fingers had touched and delved, but not nearly enough. *Cristo*, his need for her was like a madness in his blood. Even now, when they were emotionally as far from each other as they could conceivably be, he wanted her. He wanted to taste her on his tongue, to feel her writhe beneath him, to watch her find her pleasure. He could describe every single change that happened to Emily when she orgasmed.

The way that her head would fall back, her mouth would open on gasps that climbed higher and higher as she did, the way that she had learned to find ecstasy in her own sighs and cries and moans, the way that the closer she came, her breath would get caught in her lungs and she would reach for him, she would find him, her muscles quivering around him, gripping him and she would take him with her as she flew through her own orgasm.

He flicked the snap of his trousers angrily, releasing an erection he'd brought on himself from the confines of his trousers. *Por Dios*, he was supposed to be trying to fix his marriage, not lust over his wife like a naughty schoolboy. He shoved the trousers from his legs and rinsed off in the shower before grabbing a towel and hoping to hell that Emily had left his room by the time he emerged.

After he changed into clean and, more importantly, *dry* clothing he would turn his focus to the matter at hand. The goal? Convince his wife to return. Nothing else mattered.

Emily stood at the sink, gently dipping the herbal tea bag in and out of the hot water in her mug, strangely comforted by the way that Diabla wound herself back and forth through her legs. And she needed that comfort because the longer and longer that Javier took to come down from the bedroom, the worse her nerves became. It was as if six years' worth of ignoring everything had built up such a mass of tension and jumbled hurts and pains that she couldn't quite see right and she was genuinely worried at what might come out of her mouth.

All she knew was that, one way or another, things had to change. It was just that she couldn't see her way through to anything other than...

'We will not divorce.'

Javier's pronouncement startled her as much as the cat and, with a screech and a hiss, Diabla disappeared in a flash.

Hot water sloshed over the side of the mug and down the back of her hand and a stifled cry caught in her throat. Javier cursed and came to her, taking the mug from her hand and turning on the cold water tap. Ever so gently he placed her hand beneath the stream, holding it when she would have flinched away, with all the care she knew him capable of. It was one of the reasons she had fallen so hard and so fast for the Spaniard. He had an innate sense of nurture he didn't know he possessed.

He placed her palm against his own, warming her hand from beneath so that the frigid water didn't bite as much. She was surprised when he huffed out a little laugh. 'Gabi did this once. She was trying to make me coffee and she burned her hand.'

She was distracted by the way his fingers

encased her hand as if it were something truly precious. 'What did your mother do when she found out?'

His silence drew her gaze, but he was still focused on her hand—or so it seemed. Until the slightest of shakes of his head told her that his mother had done absolutely nothing. Her heart turned and she realised that she was not surprised, only more curious about Renata Casas than she had been before.

What she knew of his mother was arrogance, selfishness and disdain. But she had always presumed that came from a place of maternal snobbery—that Emily hadn't been good enough for her son. But now she was beginning to wonder if it was something else.

She was about to ask, when he turned off the tap and wrapped her hand in a clean tea towel. 'I'll get the arnica.'

She reached for him as he turned. 'Javier—'

'I mean it, *mi amore*,' he warned, his dark eyes glowing with intent. 'We will not divorce.'

And what rocked Emily more was the way her heart soared at his declaration. He returned before she could gather herself and pulled out a chair for her to take. After he sat, he reached for her hand and gently rubbed the soothing cream into her skin.

The circles his thumb made across her hand

calmed her against her will. She wanted to stay angry at him. Needed to, but the care he was giving her was undermining her intent with the same intensity as the next words that came out of his mouth.

'I meant my vows.'

'So did I.' She'd expected her words to sound defensive and was surprised when they fell between them with a sadness that was painful to her own ears.

The flex of muscle at Javier's jaw told her he'd felt it too. 'What did you mean? About me leaving?' he clarified before she could ask.

He really didn't know. Emily didn't know whether that made it better or worse.

'You were never here, Javi,' she said, pulling her hand from the warm embrace of his fingers.

He frowned. 'I was working for us—to secure our future.'

'Our future *was* secure,' she insisted gently. 'We were together.' It was all she had needed. All she had *wanted.* 'We didn't need anything else.'

She almost read the thought in his eyes. *I did.* That was what he'd intended to say. And while they couldn't, wouldn't, say these things to each other, they didn't have a future.

'We needed money, *mi vida.*'

'We already had so much. More than I could even have imagined,' she reminded him.

'We needed security, Emily. My mother will never relinquish control over Casas Textiles. My uncle had given me a small start-up business but…' he looked away as if finding it difficult to discuss these things '…but I needed to make my own way. And then when Santi was looking for investors in his film… No one would fund him. He was going to have to drop it and I couldn't let that happen. So I took a risk. I invested heavily—*too* heavily. My uncle, if he'd known, would have taken back his business, thinking me reckless. But he'd have been wrong. I *prepared* for a significant financial loss. So I worked three times as hard, all the hours I could to counter any possible loss, all in order to have something of our own.'

'Javier…' She hadn't known anything of this. Only now was she beginning to realise just how much he had kept her truly on the outside of their marriage.

'It was okay ultimately, of course,' he said, but she knew that he must have been talking about money in the millions, not thousands. The pressure and the stress must have been… *had been* considerable.

'Why didn't you say?'

'Because it was *my* responsibility,' he said, bumping the flat edge of his fist against his chest. 'It had been my choice, my decision to invest in such a risky proposition, and for me to fix.'

'But as your wife, I wanted to share that burden.'

'No. As your husband, I wanted to protect you from such things.'

She tried to stop herself from growling. 'And *that* is why I felt alone in this marriage. Because you didn't include me. You didn't share things with me—and you were so focused on money and the future that you forgot me and the present.'

'No! Everything was for you, Emily, don't you see that? I didn't forget you ever.'

'No? What about Francesca's party? What about leaving me on a private plane on the runway for three hours?'

Javier looked at her, his face a mask of confusion. 'I don't… I—'

Emily huffed out a bitter laugh. 'You didn't remember then. I don't know why I'd think you'd remember now.'

'What are you talking about?'

'I'm talking about the night you bought me the sequin dress.'

Javier clenched his teeth, pressing down

against a familiar wave of anger. He remembered that night *very* well. It was the night Santi had told him how much the revenue forecast was for the film. It had been beyond their wildest imaginations. The premiere was three days away and he'd bought Emily a dress of shimmering midnight. He wanted her at his side on the red carpet, so that he could show her it had all been worth it. So that he could show her his success. He'd got home later than he'd planned because he'd arranged for the department store to stay open so he could pick it up for her.

'But what does Francesca have to do with that?'

His wife looked at him with such hurt that an icy sweat frosted his neck.

'The night you bought me that dress was the night you had agreed to come with me to Francesca's party. The night we were supposed to fly back to England. The night I waited. And waited.' Javier's fists clenched as Emily's words became thick and her eyes shone unnaturally with unshed tears. 'I waited for three hours. And when you came home that night, barely minutes after I did, you gave me that dress and invited me to an event *you* wanted me to come to. Something that was important to *you.*'

She shook her head at him, sending a waterfall of golden hair shimmering in the late afternoon light, downplaying a hurt that he felt as his own, her pride both powerful and heartbreaking.

He desperately tried to remember it, her asking him to Francesca's party, but he couldn't. He knew that he had been drowning in work at that time, but had he made her wait like that?

'Why was the party so important?' he asked, hating that he couldn't remember the straw that had destroyed his marriage.

'Because I wanted my friends to meet you so that they would stop whispering about us and looking at me with pity as if I'd made a massive mistake.'

Cristo. 'It was *not* a mistake, Emily.'

'No? We were so young, Javi. I was nineteen, you twenty-one. We hadn't known each other more than three months when we married.'

But I'd known you only two minutes when I knew.

The concrete solid answer stayed in his mind though, that child in him still too hurt and fearful that she would leave again, not ready to say it out loud. He rubbed unconsciously at the pressure in his chest, unaware of how the action drew Emily's gaze.

'So instead of coming to the premiere of Santi's film...' He couldn't finish the sentence. He couldn't put it into words without the howling pain of her abandonment leaching from his voice. But Emily was telling him that he'd done the same to her?

'I left. I left, hoping that you would finally notice me. I didn't care about the money, Javier. I didn't need future security, I cared about us,' she said, as if she'd sensed his attempts to justify his actions.

His senses went on full alert. 'Why are you talking in the past tense, Emily?'

'Because nothing has changed. You are still making decisions based on what you want. Not us. Not me. I can't live my life as if it is all about you,' she said, the jagged hitch in her breath so telling of how difficult this conversation was for her.

Ache. That was all he felt in that moment. Radiating out from his chest, everything hurt and from somewhere deep within a panic like nothing he'd ever experienced before was telling him to grab her now before she left him again. Because if she left now, he knew, *knew*, she would never come back. His pulse raged at his temples, blood pounding his heart in a frantic drumbeat.

How had he got things so wrong? How was he here?

He would fix this. He had to. He wouldn't, *couldn't*, fail this time.

'I should go,' Emily said, pushing the chair back from the table.

'Two weeks.' The words burst out into the open. 'Give me two weeks.'

'Javier...' His name on her lips was a perverted plea, the sound so wrong, but he wouldn't bow to it.

'You owe me that much,' he said, his voice hardened.

'And then what? After two weeks, what? You'll let me go then?'

'If that is what you want.' He forced the words from his lips, knowing that it was no risk. Javier Casas never made a deal he didn't know he could win. He might have underestimated Emily, but he knew his wife, he knew what she liked, what she wanted. All he had to do was give her those things and she'd be back by his side. He would have fixed it. He wouldn't have failed. The panic began to recede as he clawed back control.

'You'll give me a divorce?'

No. 'If that is what you want,' he replied again, his hands forming fists beneath the table. *It wouldn't come to that.* He would make sure of it.

'Then I have a condition.'

He caught his response before it revealed his surprise. 'Go on,' he invited.

'We will not have sex for these two weeks.'

He choked, actually choked, on air. 'No. Emily. Be serious,' he begged.

'I am serious,' she insisted, the blush riding high on her apple-round cheeks.

'*Mi corazón*, that is crazy. What is between us is—'

'Distracting, and always has been. If we have any hope of getting to the root of our marriage problems, you can't just sex me into forgiving you.'

'Sex you into... Emily—'

'No!' She put up her hand, firm and decisive. 'You do this, Javi. You come in all handsome and determined and...' she shook her hand up at him '...and *that* and you distract me from being mad at you.'

'Emily, if it's that easy to make you *not* mad at me, maybe you weren't that mad at me in the first place?'

'That is not a reasonable argument, Javier!'

He shrugged, really not quite sure that it wasn't. And although Emily had just made it that much harder to get his wife back, she had apparently forgotten that he was most definitely a worthy opponent.

'Define sex.'

'Excuse me?' Emily squeaked, her eyes wide with shock.

He shrugged again, enjoying unsettling his wife a little too much.

'Define sex,' he repeated slowly.

'Well, you know...'

There was absolutely no way in hell he was helping her out of this one. If she wanted to make such a ridiculous stipulation to their agreement, then she was going to have to define her terms. And if it left him any leeway at all, any, he planned to make full use of it.

'Intercourse,' she finally said, the word erupting from her mouth as if she'd held her breath around it.

'Agreed,' he replied swiftly before she realised how much room to manoeuvre she'd allowed him, 'but I have a condition of my own.' Her eyes narrowed, expecting him to be up to something. Good. She would need her wits about her. 'You will share my bed.'

'But we're not having sex.'

'No,' he agreed, wondering why she thought that the two were mutually exclusive. Yes, he'd always made love to his wife every chance he got, but... He clenched his jaw against the shockingly soft turn of his heart when he remembered what it had been like to wake up with her head on his arm, the curve of her body fitting so perfectly against his, the scent of her hair on the pillow. And now he was wondering whether he should take it back.

'You want to share a bed with me even though I will not sleep with you?'

He nodded, not quite trusting himself to speak or what else he might end up saying.

'Okay,' she agreed hesitantly, gingerly stretching out her hand for him to shake.

He nearly laughed, feeling almost guilty for something that would be so easy for him to achieve. He took her small palm into his hand, ignoring the warning sizzle and heat and spark.

'It is a deal, *mi reina*.'

Javier got up from the table, startling her.

'Where are you going?' Emily asked, somewhat dazed by the events of the past hour.

'I'm going to move your things.'

She opened her mouth to argue but nothing came out. She had—undeniably—agreed to share his bed, just as he had agreed—undeniably—not to sleep with her. And only now was she realising the torment she had just consigned herself to. She dropped her forehead to the table the moment he left the room.

What on earth had she done?

She was about to call him back, call it all off, call Francesca to arrange for someone to come get her, when she heard a distinctly feline cry and a uniquely male tirade of curses. Racing upstairs, Diabla speeding the opposite way in a streak, Emily rounded the corner to the master suite and gasped.

And then she laughed. She laughed so hard she started to cry, beautiful big joyful tears rolling down her cheeks.

'Oh, my...' she managed through her hysterics, bending double at the waist to try to relieve the pressure on her stomach muscles.

Javier turned, holding up what had once been one of his most expensive shirts, but was now barely strips of material. Fluff and feathers danced in the air from the absolute destruction that was the master suite. The look on his face was a picture! Miserably, Javier picked through the mess on the floor to retrieve a pair of his favourite trousers, setting Emily off on another round of impossible to stop giggles.

He turned back to her and stared as if she'd lost her mind. 'You can laugh, *cariño*, but have you seen what she did to your curtains?'

And then she stopped laughing.

CHAPTER SEVEN

EMILY SHIFTED HER LEGS, the satiny glide of the fresh sheets she'd put on the bed late last night decadent and delicious. Warmth and comfort surrounded her and she buried herself deeper into the plush bedding. The scent of sandalwood, mint and something peppery coiled a tempting tension in her sex, low and incessant. She inhaled dreamily and then screamed when Javier shifted beside her.

'I am right here, you know. If you wanted—'

She turned and slapped him on the arm. 'You scared me!' she accused.

'I was not hiding, *mi vida*.' Javier laughed, throwing back the sheets and getting out of bed.

The sight of his nakedness made her gasp, and slam her eyelids closed as quickly as possible.

'Emily,' he chided. 'It is nothing you have not seen before.'

'Yes, but that was different.' She felt the bed dip beneath his weight, as if he were kneeling beside her.

'Mrs Casas.'

He was waiting for her to look at him—because that was her husband. He commanded, demanded, complete attention. Gingerly, she prised one eyelid open to find him but millimetres away from her. The hypnotic depths of his brown eyes, fathomless and rich enough to drown in, seduced her sleep-addled brain and she allowed him to nuzzle her head to the side, to lean into the crook of her neck and inhale deeply from her skin—an unabashed declaration of intent mocking her sleepy sips at his scent from her pillow.

'You made the rules,' he whispered, his breath fanning out against her shoulder. 'The moment you agree to return to my side, we can get rid of this silly embargo and enjoy whole *days* of making love. Believe me, *cariño*, I want nothing more.'

And with that proclamation he was gone, leaving her in a melting puddle of desire and aching frustration in the bed they now shared.

Emily was not a fool and she wasn't used to lying to herself. Of course she wanted to sleep with her husband. The man was sculpted marble come to life in hot flesh. In six years, he had only become that much bigger and stronger. Javier had always been proud of his physique, relishing the power and strength he honed through disciplined workouts and hours at the gym—it was an energy he'd needed to expel she'd realised quite early on. Not that she'd once complained because he was simply mouth-watering. The breadth of his shoulders, biceps she didn't have a hope of circling even with both hands, the ripple of abdominal muscles that concertinaed when he laughed, or when he… She stifled that thought with a yank so severe she slammed her eyes shut. Even then, she could see the whorls of dark hair across his chest, remembered the way she had stroked and teased both herself and him as she tripped downward to the powerful jut of his erection.

Emily rubbed her thighs together, unable to prevent the pulse of need flaring at her core. Behind lidded eyes, she saw him in her mind, staring at her in *that* way, his lips a perpetual pout as if daring her to find fault in anything about him—and the infuriating fact that she couldn't. That challenge, it was a drug, a lure, a trap.

Because her husband was not above using sex to get what he wanted. And Javier Casas was simply a man who did not lose. But this was one game Emily couldn't afford to take lightly. She had meant what she said the day before. Nothing had changed. Javier was still a man who, purposely or not, put his needs and desires first. Not for nefarious purposes, not for greed or ill will but almost out of sheer stubbornness. It was strange that she hadn't really seen that before. Did it help that it was a thoughtless kind of selfishness or did it make it worse? Maybe if she understood a little more why... The thought made her feel embarrassed that she didn't know her husband as well as she'd thought she had. Was it possible to fall in love with someone before you knew them? They'd been in such a rush to marry, so full of passion and urgency and youthful confidence.

'I meant my vows.'

As had she, her inner voice insisted, feeling the truth of it sinking in. And being here, in their home in Frigiliana, she remembered. She remembered all the reasons she *did* love him. The power and care, the way he'd made her laugh, the way he had drawn an inhibited girl from London into a world of passion and colour and brightness and even the early stirrings of her own power. They *had* shared that. And she would never lie. Could not lie about this. She *did* love him.

But it hadn't been enough. Because she simply couldn't be like her mother. Couldn't and wouldn't lose herself to a man so much that she forgot her own child as much as she forgot herself. And that was why Emily pulled herself together and was gone by the time Javier emerged from the bathroom.

Emily was at the table when Javier came to a halt in the kitchen doorway. Diabla was peering at him from where she wove herself between Emily's calves. He glared at the beast that had done untold damage to his wardrobe and—the gall of the animal—she glared back before darting away the moment he crossed the threshold.

He bit back the low growl in his throat, realising that he might have to put more effort into winning over Diabla than his wife. With that in mind, he placed the bottle of sunscreen on the table next to Emily's breakfast plate as he pulled out his phone to order something online that might help him with the cat.

'What is this?' Emily asked, picking up the bottle.

'It's sunscreen.'

'Clearly.'

'You need to put some on. We'll be leaving in—'

A single raised eyebrow stopped him in his

tracks and he stifled a much deeper growl this time. *Include her.* She wanted to be part of this with him. He had listened last night. He had heard what she'd said and it had cut him deep to know that he had made his wife feel so alone. He knew that feeling and never would wish it on anyone. But the rawness of that realisation, the realness of it was too much too soon. So he forced levity into his tone to hide the acid beginning to erode the rust on doors better left closed.

'Darling, I would love it if you would put on some sunscreen,' he said, pitching his tone at an alarming tooth-rotting level. 'I have somewhere that I'd like to take you and we would be leaving in about ten minutes—if that is something you would like?'

'I believe there was even a question in there, husband. I *am* impressed,' Emily responded, a light tease in her eyes, but also…a spark. A flash of joy that he had forgotten—one that lit something deep within him. Satisfaction. Peace. A joy of his own.

'Where are we going?' she asked.

'Somewhere I should have taken you a long time ago,' he admitted in a rare burst of truth.

Javier loved driving. Even the shock of the accident hadn't worn that away. The first ten minutes, settling into the car and the drive had taken a lot more of his concentration than usual. But when Emily had slipped her fingers around the death grip he had on the gear stick he had allowed himself to relax into the winding curves that would take them out and away from Frigiliana towards their destination.

With the top down on the matte grey convertible, the morning sun streamed down on them. Emily lost the battle to tame the strands of her hair and sank into the passenger seat, unable to hide her excited smile.

Shifting gears up and down to navigate the twists and turns, there was a happy silence between them, neither choosing to shout above the roar of the wind and the engine. And he wondered how long it had been since he had simply let things go. Thoughts of work, the endless turnover of meetings and emails, managing his mother from as far away as possible. The thought turned in his mind. This was the longest time Renata had been quiet. Usually by now she would have been after him for money to help prop up the business she seemed determined to drive headlong into the ground.

He felt Emily's fingers brush against his again, and forced himself to let go of the tension that had built shockingly fast. In the last few years his mother had been affecting him more and more. Whether it was because she was asking for more or whether over the years the weight of her had accumulated to become heavier and heavier, he didn't know. He pasted a smile on his face as he turned to Emily, just as she saw the turnoff sign for their destination.

She leaned up in the seat and turned to stare at him. 'Really?' she asked and suddenly he felt awful. Awful that she was so pleased by such a small thing.

'Really,' he insisted, promising silently to never make her wait for anything she desired ever again.

As they turned the corner, a pounding joy thumped in her chest. Emily had wanted to visit the Alhambra since she'd first come to Spain, yet somehow in the whirlwind of her romance with Javier it had never happened. But as they pulled into an empty car park Emily's heart dropped. She tried to tell herself not to be disappointed but, from the absolute quietness, it didn't look as if it would happen today. Notorious for mile-long queues and renowned for only high, very high, or extreme periods of activity, the empty car park was clearly a sign of closure.

'What is wrong?' Javier asked, seemingly unaware of the situation.

'Is it a bank holiday today?'

'No.' He frowned, confused. 'Why?'

Emily shrugged. 'It's a shame to have come all this way and for it to be closed.'

'It's not closed,' he replied easily as he got out of the car, came round and opened her door for her.

'Javier, there's no one here.'

He looked at her as if she were being obtuse. '*You* are here.'

Javier led them away from the large stone arch that formed the main entrance before she could read the signs placed across the door and towards a small man in a uniform. A regal bow greeted them and the staff member beckoned them through a side door.

Javier begged just a minute from her and disappeared with the older man, while Emily turned in a circle in the dusty courtyard that was surrounded by such incredible beauty. The Alhambra had been a military fortress and a royal palace, displaying both Islamic architecture and that of the Spanish Renaissance. The different styles juxtaposed should have created chaos, but instead it was a work of art.

She bathed in the warm earthy glow of the walls that had inspired the name of the sprawling building, The Red One. Perched up high on the hill, the exterior of the walled palaces appeared no less regal for its martial purpose. But it was the interior of the Nasrid Palaces that drew her—the intricate tiling, mosaics, carved wood and, her favourite, the mirador—arcaded porticos that brought the stunning view outside *in*. Here, the city of Granada, or the world-renowned gardens, appeared as if they were a piece of artwork displayed in the room.

She felt her creative well being filled with each breath and each new sight—creeping into her soul and feeding her heart. To be here—alone…it was as incredible as it was inconceivable. That Javier had done this—that he'd *remembered*…

'Well?' he asked, the crunch of his shoes on the gravel behind her alerting her to his presence long before his words. Beside him a young woman held a tray with flutes of champagne, glasses of what looked like fresh lemonade and small plates of tapas, exquisite enough to make her salivate.

She shared a delighted look with Javier and took a glass of lemonade and a few tapas, trying to swallow around the smile that pulled at her lips as Javier fussed over his choice. Finally satiated, he took a lemonade and, turning away from the staff member, he gestured towards the ancient buildings. 'Where shall we start?'

He had taken his sunglasses off, twirling them loosely in his hand, his head cocked to one side and a look of pure indulgence in his eyes. His white shirt, open at the collar, folded back at the sleeves, only served to highlight the bronze of his skin—already losing the unhealthy grey pallor from the accident. The bruise on his cheek was barely showing and the fall of his dark hair covered the stitches he'd received from the cut on his head. A different kind of excitement warmed her now. Heat in his gaze, an eyebrow raised as if sensing the direction of her thoughts.

'You know, we are completely alone, *cariño*...'

Frowning, she looked behind her to see that the woman had disappeared and she tried and failed—again—to stop the smile from pulling at her lips. 'You're incorrigible.'

'You started it,' he happily threw back, holding out the crook of his arm like a Victorian gentleman.

This. She'd missed it. The teasing, the lightness, the way the fun back and forth made her feel younger, happier, free. The years after she'd left Javier had been dark and heavy and hard. And being the boss of the small team meant that she'd had to make difficult decisions and pull rank occasionally. It hadn't exactly made space for...fun.

She took his arm and looked up at her husband. 'We can go anywhere?'

'Anywhere.'

'And it's just us?'

'Just us.'

She knew exactly where to start. She led Javier towards the Nasrid Palaces that had first caught her attention in school and held it, but even that years-long infatuation couldn't prevent the question that had been waiting impatiently on the tip of her tongue.

'Javi,' she whispered, 'just how rich *are* you?'

He looked at her for a moment, then threw his head back and laughed. Big, loud, joyous laughter that confused but delighted her.

'Very, is the short answer,' he managed with a rueful smile when he had just about recovered.

Emily, no wiser, simply waited and Javier nodded once and looked up over to the Sierra Nevada mountain range in the distance.

'No one expected Santi's film to be such a roaring success. Not even us.'

'If it was such a shot in the dark, why did you do it?'

'Because Santi is my brother,' he said simply. 'Not by blood, no, but we've known each other since we were six years old when we went first went head to head in the playground.'

'Who won?' she asked, entranced by the image of the two powerful, handsome men she knew as children.

'*Cariño*, you have to ask?' Javier scolded.

'Santi then,' she concluded in a tease.

He smiled begrudgingly before the smile dimmed a little. 'It was a huge gamble though. *Huge*,' he repeated as if he was still shocked by it even now. 'But it wasn't just because Santi had asked,' he admitted. 'I needed something that wasn't from Gael, or Renata. Something that couldn't be taken away on a whim. I needed to *succeed*.'

And for the first time in six years Emily felt the stirring of understanding deep within her. No, back then she wouldn't have understood. But now that she had her own business, poured blood, sweat and tears into it, she knew the sense of self it provided, the confidence, but she was surprised to hear that he'd needed to feel it too.

'And when Santi's film made over one hundred million at the box office...'

Javier opened his hand to the sky and shrugged. 'It was an incredible windfall. I invested again with Santi but also in other things. Over the years, I have lost some money but made an incredible amount more. Now I work with a group of people to try and put as much of that money back into the world as possible, but yes. I still have a lot of money.'

Emily knew Javier well enough to know that it was less about money and more about reaching that private, secret internal goal he'd set for himself. He had always been driven, in every single thing he did. Driven to a point of ruthlessness that bordered on selfishness. The thought turned something in her chest as they made their way towards the heart of the Alhambra.

'It is amazing what you have achieved, Javier. Really,' she said, her palm resting on the bare skin of his forearm sending sparks right to his chest. 'The success you have become is incredible.' His wife's simple words struck him with the full force of a punch that stopped his heart. His mind flatlined at the realisation that no one had ever said that to him. They had celebrated it, desired it, envied it more often than not. But recognising his achievements… Emily looked at him with silver sparks in her blue eyes that were all the more powerful for not being sensual. And then…

'Your mother must be happy,' she said ruefully.

Javier looked away. 'She doesn't know.'

Emily frowned, her steps stalling a little. 'What do you mean?'

'It is better that she doesn't know.'

Renata was a black hole that he could pour money into for the rest of his life and she'd never be satisfied. Whether it was for the business she'd inherited from her father, or for herself, money made Renata's cruelty vicious, the memory of it passing a cold shadow across the warmth of the morning.

But he knew that Emily deserved more of an explanation than that. So there, despite the gentle burn of the morning sun against his skin, he chose to walk into ice.

'She is...' he struggled for words that were honest, despite the familial guilt that nipped at the truth '...dangerously selfish. Oh, she can be gregarious and dramatic to the point of comedy—' he gentled his words with a small smile '—but beneath that is something...much more complex.'

He could see that his oblique descriptions were not enough to clear the confusion in Emily's eyes and suddenly he wanted her to understand, as much as he feared that understanding. He led her to a bench and gestured for her to sit.

'You asked me what food my mother made for me when I was sick as a child. We weren't allowed to be sick,' he said, swallowing the memories. 'It would either interfere with her plans or take the focus from her. We were told we were simply not ill and with such conviction...' He shook his head, marvelling even today how he had tried so hard to believe her. 'On the surface I imagine we looked like a happy family. But her thirst for attention was, *is*, unquenchable. It is worse when she is unmarried.' He clenched his jaw and his neck corded with tension, stifling the emotions that rose to the surface. 'And if we do not give her the attention she craves, she becomes harsh and vicious and unbearably cruel. But if we do, then she is *lavish*. She can pour love and attention on you. Before Gabi was born Renata would pull me out of school and we would go on luxurious holidays to Greek islands and the Caribbean. She would dress me in suits and teach me to dance. How to be a proper man. To bring her gifts and compliment her in just the right way.'

'What about your father?'

'He left before my second birthday, after nearly running Casas Textiles into the ground. Over the years, every time I made a mistake, or got something wrong, she told me I was just like him. A failure. For my entire childhood, I walked on the edge of making a mistake.' He was surprised when Emily uncurled the hand that had unconsciously formed a fist and slipped her fingers through his. She swept his hair back and cupped the side of his face. He captured her hand before it could do any more damage to his already weak defences.

'I would cut ties with her if I could...'
'But?'

Javier shook his head. 'Gabi. I cannot leave her to Renata's whims.' His jaw seemed clenched so tight, Emily was almost surprised when he spoke again. 'I asked her to come and live with me once. Gabi,' he clarified. The tension in Javier's body told her how hard it was for him to admit this. It was clear that his sister had chosen to stay with Renata—as clear as the emotional toll her decision had taken on Javier. The rejection of it must have been a devastating blow. He shook his head. 'For now the only way I can protect Gabi is by giving Renata the money she asks for, keeping her happy.'

Emily's heart ached for him. She couldn't imagine feeling constantly held hostage by a parent, never knowing what to expect from the one constant that should be inviolate.

'But I fear that, in doing so, I've allowed her to become a monster.'

Emily shook her head at him. 'Javi,' she chided gently. 'You are her son, not her father or husband. You are not her equal and you are not her keeper,' she said gently. 'Her behaviour is not on you.'

He shook off her words and her reassurance. Emily didn't understand, couldn't. Yes, Renata had been abhorrent, but she was still his mother. She—unlike his father—had at least stayed. A flash of anger was unleashed and spread outwards with shocking intensity and swirled around the Emily who had also left, but he yanked it back with a ferocity that had him snapping his head up.

As if sensing that her words had not been heard, she turned back to look at the entrance to the Nasrid Palaces. 'Perhaps there is still time to do something for Gabi.'

Javier nodded, his jaw aching from keeping too much in.

'And maybe there is also a chance to change the way things are with Renata. Not her, I don't think that will happen,' Emily admitted, 'but perhaps you can change the way that you deal with her. Changing what you give her might mean you change what you get from her.'

His mind caught on her words but he wasn't ready to follow that statement through, so instead he followed her gaze to the sun-touched pinky-red richness of the buildings.

'So, are we talking *billions*? Because if so…'

A bark of laughter erupted unbidden but welcome into the morning sunshine, lifting the anvil-heavy weight from his chest, making it something more bearable.

Emily tugged him from the bench and began explaining the history of a site he knew well but was happy to hear. Gently, easily, she described how the different influences had come to create what could easily be one of the Wonders of the Modern World.

He followed her as she entered Casa Real Vieja—the Old Royal Palace as opposed to the newer palaces erected during the Christian Spanish period of development. Each of the three palaces—Mexuar, the Comares Palace and the Palace of the Lions—was exquisite, and detailed with such intricacy he was mesmerised. But it was his wife that drew his gaze.

She had drifted away from his hold, eyes wide with awe and emotion as she moved slowly through each and every room. The sense of peace and serenity he felt as they moved on a stream of Emily's desire and curiosity, her surprised gasps of joy at something small but beautiful, the way she tugged at him to see what she saw, the way she shared her enthusiasm and excitement with him… He had missed all this because he had been too stubborn.

No. She had denied them this. She had taken this all away from him when she'd left.

He wrestled with the voice that sounded far too much like his mother, and far too much like the child who had been deserted by his father, lashing out in the face of such devastating abandonment. So he stifled it, thrusting it down, ignoring the hurt that the memories of his childhood had evoked, desperate not to be that lost, lonely boy again. His head began to hurt as his mind and soul veered between what had happened in the past and what he wanted from the future.

At that moment, Emily drifted towards an open archway that looked out at the incredible vista beyond. The interior of the chamber, shrouded in darkness with only natural light pouring through intricately detailed carving, made it appear as if the sun itself reached for her. The outline of her figure, the calf-length skirt nipped in at the waist a V-neck blouse was tucked into, and the way she had tucked her foot behind the ankle of her other leg hit him with such a strange blow—one of *jamais vu*.

He had seen her stand like that a thousand

times, but this was the first that felt unfamiliar and out of reach. A cold sweat broke out across the back of his neck and a panicked pulse fluttered in his veins. The strange sense morphed into a certainty. As if he knew that this was his last chance to get it right or lose her for ever.

CHAPTER EIGHT

NEARLY A WEEK had gone by since they had visited the Alhambra, and Emily was both exhausted and inspired. Javier had taken her across Spain to visit some of the most incredible places, museums, galleries; anywhere she had ever mentioned a desire to visit, they had gone.

During the day they would feast upon Gaudí and Rothko, Jorge Oteiza and Eduardo Chillida, visiting the Guggenheim Bilbao and exhibitions at the Centre Pompidou Málaga, while in the evenings they would discover a world of culinary delights from Michelin starred restaurants to side-street vendors, delectable tapas to seven-course wine-tasting menus.

It was glorious, truly, and Emily could already feel the inspiration scratching at her, waiting to come out. So she had snatched the few hours Javier would allow himself to recuperate—his energy still startlingly low from the accident—to throw herself into her work as much as possible. Her team were doing wonderfully, and the energy and inspiration she felt at being here, seeing what she was seeing, allowed her to focus her creativity to the point where she was producing some of the best work she had done in the last few years.

The team missed her, but they were happy and busy. *She* was happy and busy...but it couldn't stop her mind circling back to what Javier had said when he'd opened up to her about his mother. He had shown her a childhood of hurt and neglect, with sporadic freedom in school or when his mother was occupied with a distraction. But, combining his descriptions with her own experience of Renata Casas and Emily had realised that the level of narcissism she portrayed was not a characteristic, but a very real trait. The kind of damage a person with such a brutally selfish world view could do to those around them, let alone a child...

As shocking as it had been, it had provided a real insight into him, allowing her to form an understanding of him that she'd never had before. She could see how he must have had to cling so incredibly tight onto his needs, his desires, to not lose them in the face of his mother's forceful personality. How hard he must have had to work to ensure that his wants were not obliterated by her demands. Perhaps so hard that he still clung to his needs with a strength that was too much sometimes. That understanding of him made her feel close to him...just as he seemed to be pulling away again. Since that day he'd kept her too busy to think, let alone ask any further questions. Questions that, she forced herself to admit, she was afraid to ask.

'What about your father?'

'He left...'

The two words had struck hard, leaving a shadow word ringing in her ear. *Abandoned.* Like, she was sure, Javier had felt when Gabi chose to stay with his mother. And exactly like he must have felt when she had left him six years ago. Guilt twisted her stomach into knots. But she had done so not knowing the whole story at the time. So no, Emily wouldn't blame herself for the decisions she'd made then.

But she *could* take responsibility for the decisions she made about the man she encountered now. He was as alluring, if not more so, than he had ever been. And, despite the caution she felt, she was swept up by her husband all over again. It was the little things that got to her. Three days ago, she had come down into the living room to find him reading a book. When she'd asked what it was, he'd tilted the cover for her to see—*Bald but Beautiful: Everything you need to know about Sphynx Cats*—tersely informing her that he was 'getting to know' his enemy. That his supposed enemy had started to follow him round the house was not something she felt like pointing out. Of course, it had nothing to do with the little trail of treats he would leave for Diabla even as he gently ignored her. Though it was less ignoring and more like gentling her in to his presence. Even if they visited the other side of Spain, Javier would make sure they returned that evening, no matter the time, because *he preferred their bed*. But she knew it was because he didn't like leaving Diabla alone for that long.

Yet, despite all his outward charm and attention, there was a sense of tension in Javier that Emily couldn't quite put her finger on. It was as raw and powerful and deeper than any tension she'd felt between them before. It was an undercurrent that both drew her and scared her, not physically but emotionally, and Emily was beginning to realise that with Javier that was perhaps the more dangerous of the two.

She knew she had been right to put that barrier between them—if she slept with Javier, if she made love with her husband, she feared she would be irrevocably lost. And he'd kept his word and not tried to sleep with her. But that didn't prevent the magnetic draw she felt to him, it didn't stop her from reacting when his hand lay upon her hip in the morning, gently tugging her back into the aroused warm body that thrummed with the same need, the same desires that whispered beneath her skin. It didn't help her heart and the way it jerked and pulsed and stopped and tripped when he emerged from the shower with a towel around his waist, or when he looked at her as if she were the only person in the entire world and he was just fine with that. Just a hint of that sandalwood scent, crushed mint and peppercorn, and her body softened, her defences melted just that little bit more.

And on a night like this, when he had covered the patio in tea lights, set champagne in an ice bucket, lit incense so that its heady scented smoke uncurled exotic thoughts and gentle music played from inbuilt speakers he was even harder to resist.

'You are trying to seduce me,' she accused as he came out onto the patio, Diabla weaving through his legs, both with such feline grace that neither tripped. If he was aware of just how much he'd won over the little she-devil, he showed no sign of it. Emily hid her smile in the turn of her head towards the champagne.

'But of course. What kind of husband would I be not to do so?' he asked, the charm present, but not quite able to mask that tense bass note in his voice.

'Is everything okay?' Emily asked, trying to ignore that feeling of once again being shut out by her husband.

'Of course, *mi reina.*'

He was lying again. He knew it. He was pretty sure she knew it too. But this feeling...he hadn't been able to shake it since the Alhambra. And it was *horrible.* A strange, angry frustration that he couldn't release. It was branded in his soul—and God knew Javier wasn't one for the dramatic, but that was the only way he could describe it.

She joined him at the patio's balcony and he hated that she could read him so easily, but also not at all. She reached up her hand to cup his cheek, her eyes asking to be let in, but his heart was bruised enough to deny her entry.

He turned his face to her palm, laying a kiss in the centre and reaching up to her wrist to feel the flicker of her pulse against the pad of his thumb. *Cristo*, she came alive beneath his touch. It was a temptation too far. His inner voice called him a coward but his stubborn nature ignored it bluntly and willingly hurling him into a course of action that would delight them both. He had agreed to her terms and, gentleman that he was, he would not break them. But that didn't mean she hadn't left him a leeway that he was determined to make absolute and full use of.

He swept his tongue out across the pulse point and felt the ripple of goosebumps across the skin of her forearm. Her fingers curled reflexively and the whisper of pleasure that fell from her lips was only encouragement.

'Javier,' she warned half-heartedly, 'we have a deal.'

'We do,' he agreed, even as his own arousal hardened to the point of near pain.

'We shouldn't be doing this,' she said, even as her body angled towards his like a flower seeking the sun.

He pulled back just enough to look into his wife's eyes, to see, read and know her desires, those on the surface and those much deeper. And the complexity of the layers in those depths, not just need, want and arousal, but warmth, comfort and connection and the yearning for more was what sent him deeper into this madness.

'Intercourse.'

'What?' The word was a choked laugh from his wife as he bent his head to place more and more kisses along her bare arm, closing the distance between them.

'You defined sex as intercourse. It was—may I say—rather unimaginative of you, Emily,' he teased gently, reluctantly pulling back to look at her. 'But I am not such a monster that I will take control from you—unless you will it of course.'

Stormy eyes sparked white heat at his words, and what had started out as pure distraction became an irrefutable need.

'One word from you will stop me,' he said, pulling her against him, the heat of her body raising the essence of her, jasmine and orange, filling his senses and driving him wild with torment.

'Stop me, Emily,' he all but begged, knowing that this would break the last thread of his control. He pressed his forehead against hers. She knew he was distracting her. He could read the accusation in her eyes as if she had said it out loud. But desire and desperation kept her silent long enough for him to press an open mouth kiss just above her collarbone and suck so that she melted in his arms enough for him to sweep her off her feet.

He carried her over to the chair, knowing

that if they went inside, the deal, his honour and her clothes would be in tatters on the floor within seconds. He arranged her in his lap, her thighs naturally falling either side of his, and he gloried in having her above him. Her hair hung down in curtains, shielding them from the rest of the world—a glorious place where touch was erotic and thoughts were of nothing other than sin.

He drew her down against his erection, the delectable friction delighting them both as moans of need tangled in their tongues as they kissed. He promised her silently that he would keep to her deal—too much hung in the balance to not. But that didn't mean that he would let her go this night without punishing her in the most delicious of ways.

She hadn't helped matters, of course. The deceptively simple dress she was wearing had been designed with his torture in mind. The thin straps holding up the simple satin dress allowed the V at her neck to display the palm-sized flat between Emily's breasts in an invitation he couldn't refuse. He placed his hand there, against her sternum, even as his other hand slipped between the thigh-high cut in the satiny material, reaching behind her to pull her even closer, harder, deeper in a way that could never be enough to satiate his hunger for her.

He gripped and pressed, so that Emily would never know how much his hands shook with the intensity of his need for her. For this. Sheltered in the curtains of her hair, it didn't matter that he was blind with lust, he didn't need his eyes to feel, to touch, to taste.

His lips found hers with unerring accuracy and *devoured* in a roar of passion. His tongue thrust deeply into her open-mouthed acceptance. Positioned above him should have placed him at a disadvantage but he continued to possess, consume, *own* her mouth in the most exploitative of ways. And she let him. She simply opened herself to him as he sought to hide himself in her.

And that thought alone had him stopping. He shouldn't be doing this. No matter how much he wanted to, this was exactly why she had made the deal in the first place. Because he did this, used sex to distract her. And it was a line he didn't want to cross. He shifted his hands to her upper arms, trying to hold her in place when she would so willingly have closed the distance between them.

'Emily,' he said gently, trying to stop it before they lost themselves completely.

Emily shook her head. She knew that he was trying to stop this, but she didn't want him to.

They were skating so close to the edge of the deal they'd made, and she knew it was madness to do so, but she was unsettled by the tension that had worked its way from Javier into her. Emily was as angry at him as he seemed angry at her, both too fearful of speaking a truth that would or could change everything.

So, instead, she was choosing this. Choosing to burn away her frustration in the most incendiary of ways. Choosing him and knowing that while it was cowardly it was also exactly what she needed. She kissed her name from his lips, teasing open his mouth and taking full advantage when he succumbed. The groan building in the back of his throat vibrated through her body until it flared deep within her, beckoning her thighs to open just that bit more, to press against him just that bit more, to demand from him *just that bit more*.

His head fell back in a surrender she knew better than to trust. But the cords of his exposed neck were too irresistible to her. She kissed and gloried in the taste of him, salt, spice and sweet, nipping at the muscles and shuddering at the little sharp points of stubble that had grown during the day—delighting in the scratch of it against her soft skin.

His fingers flexed around her biceps, neither pulling nor pushing, but the restraint was enough, the boundary—like the confines of their deal—something she wanted to push against, to test the limit of, to know his, to understand her own.

She pushed forward, letting him keep the steel bands of his hands at her arms, returning her lips to his, laving the lush fullness of his mouth with her tongue, tormenting him with little kisses and teasing their arousal into something fierce.

Her hand went to his shoulder, fisting his shirt and grazing the muscles and skin beneath with her nails. In response his hand fisted the flesh of her backside, and a gasp of pure pleasure poured from her mouth to his. His inhalation was swift and deep, as if he were desperate to consume even her very breath, as if it were the most of her that he'd allow himself.

The thought had her almost cry out in protest, in denial. 'I want this,' she whispered desperately against his lips. 'I asked you before and that time I ran away,' she confessed, breathless and eyes closed. 'I'm asking again, and I beg you, please. Please don't stop this. Not this time. Not now.'

She knew it was selfish. She knew what she was asking, but the need for him was a madness in her blood. Gingerly she prised open her eyes to find him looking at her solemnly.

It was a moment of stillness, the eye of the storm—his gaze searching for answers she didn't know how to give—the power of his focus, she feared, would penetrate to her soul.

'This is what you want?' he asked, his hand rising to sweep back a lock of hair that had fallen forward between them.

She folded her top lip beneath her teeth and bit down, nodding. *So much.* She wanted it so damn much she dared not speak it.

'*Me rindo,*' he whispered. *I surrender.* And he was looking at her as if there was no one else in the world.

His words lifted the leash holding Emily back and she claimed his mouth with such possession they would each remember that exact moment for the rest of their lives. Hands fisted in satin and cotton, tongues teased and tasted, lips parted and pressed, sighs and growls merged as they gave and took more of each other than ever before.

Javier held her in his arms as he rose, his display of strength enthralling, and while she might seem at his mercy, she knew he was utterly at hers. He guided her down onto the cloth-covered table, gently laying her across the surface like a dying man's last meal. Emily lifted her knees, rested her feet flat onto the table and watched her husband devour her with his eyes.

'*Tu eres mi reina,*' he vowed, his determined words fanning the flames between them.

She translated the Spanish in her mind and heart. She was his queen.

His hands pressed against the satin of her dress at her calves, sweeping easily upwards as he reached her knees and parted her thighs. Her sex pulsed with desperate longing, and nothing could appease it but him. He made space for himself between her legs, bringing the hem of her dress further and further upwards, sweeping circles with his fingers through the material in a silken caress, the whisper-soft touch delicately arousing with devastating effect.

He tormented her with his gaze, showing her in his eyes exactly what he wanted to do to her, warning her, building her anticipation, his silence more effective than any words ever could have been, in there a question—a warning. A line about to be crossed and, heaven help her, she consented with a desperate nod.

Bending, he pressed a kiss to her knee, smoothing the satin aside so that lips touched flesh, tongue tasted skin, fingers gripped and held. Her eyes drifted closed and she lost herself to Javier and the sensations he was raining down on her. His kisses drew closer and closer to the juncture of her thighs, the sensual anticipation sharp and tangy in her throat and fluttering in her chest. The sound of her breath panting from her lips, the gentle growl of delight from Javier as he pressed her thighs wider, only for her knees to fall aside and her hips to lift ever so slightly... It should have been embarrassing, it should have made her feel exposed and self-conscious but, in reality, it made her feel glorious. *Sensual.* An ownership over her own desires she had never let herself feel before.

Incomprehensible words fell from Javier's lips, but she didn't need to translate them. She felt it too. There was something about this moment that surpassed any other they'd shared before. As if the truth, the deal...these past few days had stripped away layers to expose a raw honesty that they had been too young to face all those years ago.

And then he kissed her through the satin strip of her panties, his hot wet tongue finding hot wet heat and all thought burned in a pyre of passion.

For a man who was not particularly religious, Javier had never before called to God so many times in such a short space of time. But, honestly, this moment was being burned into his soul and he felt every second of it. His tongue laved her through her underwear as her thighs quivered against the table, his palm on her abdomen, not just holding her in place but savouring every twist and turn of her body, relishing the way that pleasure rippled through his wife with pride and delight.

But it wasn't enough. Sweeping the material aside, Javier pressed an open mouth kiss to the flesh beneath the blonde cross-hatch of curls. Emily nearly came off the table and he couldn't help but smile—she had always been passionate and expressive but there was something different tonight. Unable to help himself, he teased her clitoris with his tongue, pressing against it firm and hard, relishing the answering pressure Emily provided, before little licks had her writhing beneath him.

Her arousal was like a fist around his erection—an exquisite torment. One that would not see release this night. Instead, he focused the entirety of his considerable attention on bringing her to orgasm. His thumb pressed gently at her entrance was the only warning he gave before he thrust his fingers into her at the same time as he drew his tongue against her clitoris.

Emily came up off the table with a cry. His name on her lips made him ache, but the one thing he would not do that night was break their deal. He had never wanted anything or anyone as badly as he did his wife, but he knew what was at stake and he couldn't, wouldn't, risk it.

Instead, he filled her with as much passion as he could, finding that place deep within her that brought Emily more pleasure than she could contain. He teased her, pressing her towards the brink of orgasm again and again until her pleas and sobs were indelibly imprinted on his tongue. And just as she promised that she couldn't take any more, he thrust his fingers deep and hard at the same moment as he nipped at her clitoris and Emily came apart on his tongue, pulsing around his fingers and sinking into a bliss he had been honoured to give her.

Wrecked. He had wrecked them both. Shaking off his stolen languor, he gathered her into his arms and, ignoring the pull at his damaged ribs and surrounding muscles, he took her to their bed, careful of Diabla weaving around his feet. Emily attempted a sleepy protest but he removed the simple satin dress and pulled the cover over her, not even telling Diabla off when she jumped onto the bed and made a little nest in the space between Emily's knees and elbows. He didn't know how long he stayed there, just watching his wife like that, but he knew that it was too long.

Emily woke, her body still rippling with gentle pleasure despite being thoroughly satiated. She smiled at the warm bundle that was Diabla, curled up in the small curve of her body. But behind her was nothing but the coolness of the night.

She turned, glancing at the clock to find that it was three in the morning, and a sense of wrongness filled her. It tasted a little like the tension she had felt from Javier since the Alhambra. Emily knew that if she left it, if she pretended it wasn't there, Javier would never explain it, stubborn man that he was. But then, perhaps she was the coward who let him stay like that, she thought as a tendril of sadness unwound from her heart.

Gently—so that she didn't disturb Diabla—she peeled back the covers, found her robe and made her way back downstairs. The house, shrouded in darkness and lit only by moonbeams, took on a different feel. Here in the living room she could see how jarring the changes she had made to their home were. She'd expected to find Javier asleep on a chair but, when she didn't, unease crept across her skin in goosebumps. If it hadn't been for the moon glow on his white shirt, Emily would have missed him sitting out on the patio.

She watched him for longer than she should, trying to find her courage, because instinctively she knew that whatever was said next could be a far more damaging line than the sexual one she had placed between them.

'I meant my vows.'

She had too. But she had also meant what she'd said about divorce. Because neither of them could continue to live like this. She opened the door to the patio and, on bare feet, made her way over to where Javier sat on the steps that went down to the lower pool level. He didn't move, not even a millimetre, but she knew he was aware of her there. It was the imperceptible change—as if he became even more still.

She opened her mouth to speak but his words cut her off.

'Why didn't you come back?'

CHAPTER NINE

EMILY WAS GLAD that he didn't look at her when he asked. Glad that she couldn't read the expression behind the toneless question. But still her breath shivered from her lungs as she exhaled the hurt and guilt from the question.

This. This was what she had been hiding from for the last six years. She could tell herself that Javier had left her feeling lonely, had thrown himself into his business, but really... that was only half the story. And the lesser half at that.

She took a seat beside him on the step, not touching, but close enough to feel the warmth from his body. Barely hours before, she had felt stripped to raw honesty and she knew that she couldn't, wouldn't, betray him now by lying. They both deserved the truth now.

'Mum met Steven when I was about eleven,' she began, knowing it wasn't where he'd expected her answer to take them. She felt his gaze turn to her, but it was easier to look out into the shadowed gorge beyond. 'Before that, it had just been the two of us but I'd been happy with that. Mum...didn't know who my father was—she'd been seventeen when I was conceived. Angry at parents who stifled and disapproved of her, and looking for love in some very wrong places,' Emily said with a shrug, less embarrassed and more sad for her mother, who had been rejected doubly when she'd told her parents she was pregnant. 'They kicked her out.'

She heard the disdainful 'tut' which—for Javier—was expressive enough and she smiled ruefully.

'But I never felt the loss of it. Mum made everything magical. There were always stories of fairies, and parties and magic and colour. So much colour,' Emily said, remembering a childhood covered in glitter, finger-paints, mud pies and fun. The laughter and love of the years they'd spent—just the two of them—had been so, so precious to her.

'Not that it wasn't hard for her,' Emily said, nodding. 'She worked as much as she could— taking me with her on cleaning jobs until I was old enough for daycare and school. Money was...' she searched for a word that a billionaire like him would understand '...not there,' she settled on. 'But Mum made that work too. Though I saw how stressed she was when she thought I wasn't looking. The way she would bite her nails down to the quick. The way that she would drink hot water sometimes instead of lunch or have porridge for dinner. Things were hard without support from her parents and a kid at seventeen? It hadn't exactly broadened her social life. So, when she met Steven...'

The first thing Emily remembered was her mother's relief. Relief that she could share her burden. And although her mother would be devastated if she knew Emily had felt herself as such, she had. So Emily had promised herself that she'd make an effort with Steven.

'He made Mum happy. She found security with him.'

A security that had been the last thing on Emily's mind the morning of her wedding to Javier. That free-falling, reckless, *dangerous* feeling had been anything but safe. And, deep down, she'd revelled in the difference between her and her mother's wedding. Turning before the memory and the thought could take hold, she went back to what had really been behind her leaving Javier six years ago.

'I really wanted her to be happy,' she said truthfully. 'And I really didn't want to be the spoilt only child, jealous of her mum's new partner.' A tear escaped and rolled slowly down her cheek. Feeling shame and hating that it still hurt, hating the fact that she *had been* jealous.

'Mum changed. Slowly at first. Bit by bit she lost some of the colour she had brought to my childhood. I watched her losing little pieces of who she was to a man who didn't care.' An ache in her chest made the last words almost a whisper.

'It's not that Steven demands it or expects that she puts him first, but in some ways it's worse that he simply lets it happen. He takes and takes and takes and Mum won't stop. She orbits him like a moon around a planet,' Emily explained, her breath hitching in her throat. 'And that's what I feared I was doing with you.'

Emily's words hit Javier like a gut punch and a part of him regretted even asking the question. Earlier that evening he'd been so full of anger and resentment that it had felt like a poison running through his veins. Now, he'd almost welcome that feeling because it would be better than *this*.

'Emily—'

She held up her hand to stop him. 'I… It wasn't your fault, Javier. And I'm not blaming you,' she said quickly enough for him to believe it. 'But I didn't speak Spanish, and I didn't know anyone here. I put my degree on hold to stay here and my world became about you. It became waiting for you to come home, to have weekends with you so that I could talk to you and, even then, I had nothing to share other than what I'd maybe bought for the house or what I'd cooked that day.'

Javier frowned, confused and still defensive enough to sound it. 'I asked if you wanted to apply to college here.'

'You did,' she agreed, 'but I wasn't sure how much I'd get to learn without speaking the language.'

'You could have taken classes.'

'Yes…but you liked me to travel with you when you did business. I was due to start classes locally when we went to Seville for a week.'

'Yes, but—'

'And then the term after, we went to Zaragoza.'

Javier kept his mouth shut before he suggested something else that she refuted. He hadn't realised that he had done that. In fact, he disliked intensely looking back and realising that he hadn't even been aware of it at the time.

'Time just started to slip away from us and

more and more you were working and I was left behind. And I thought if I returned to England and you came after me, I'd *know*. I'd know that you saw me. I'd know that it wasn't just me that revolved around you.'

I'd know that you loved me.

He heard the words she never said and, deep within him, he felt something start to shake, to tremble under the hurt and the pain they had both borne in silence.

'Why didn't you come for me?' she asked in a small voice.

He clenched his jaw, his teeth almost cracking under the pressure. 'I couldn't,' he said, ashamed of himself now.

'Why?'

'Because,' he said, the truth gravel in his throat, 'I had failed you,' he admitted finally and the anchor tying him to guilt and anger and grief loosened a little. 'All those years of desperately trying to succeed and when it came to the most important thing in my life—*you*—I had failed. And I couldn't face the possibility of seeing that when you looked at me,' he said, closing his eyes against the wave of pain as the soul-deep truth came out. 'So I didn't. Because if I didn't see it, if I didn't come and find you, then it hadn't happened. I hadn't failed you and you hadn't left me.'

He felt her hand cup his jaw and gently turn him to face her. She waited for him to open his eyes and, when he did, he saw the same complexity of understanding, guilt, forgiveness and hurt that gripped his heart in a vice. In the silence Emily placed her head on his shoulder and they stayed that way until dawn crested the gorge, burning away the darkness and pouring gold across blue, neither moving until Diabla howled at them for denying her breakfast.

Three hours later, after feeding Diabla and falling into bed, exhausted and sleep-deprived, there was adrenaline-inducing pounding on the door. Javier cursed viciously as Emily sprang up from the bed, worried that whoever it was would smash down the door. Still groggy from the emotional revelations the night before, it took a moment for Emily to collect her thoughts.

She looked across at Javier, who had thrown off the sheet and stalked from the room in a pair of black cotton trousers, trying to ignore the heat she felt from watching the way the muscles across his back shifted as he rolled his shoulders as if readying for a fight.

Bang, bang, bang, bang, bang...

The sound shot out like bullets, startling her all over again.

Javier yelled at the door and a shout came back, quick and hot, Emily just about catching, *'Abrete, bastardo,'* before Javier fired back something that would make the devil blush.

Emily was standing at the top of the stairs by the time Javier pulled the door open to reveal Santiago, hanging from the door frame, a bottle of champagne spilling onto the courtyard floor.

'Cristo, Santi, what time is it?' Javier demanded.

'Time for drinking, *hermano,*' Santi replied, before pushing his way into the house. He came to an abrupt stop when he caught sight of her at the top of the stairs and spread his arms open in welcome. 'Emily! *Mi hermosa!* It is so good to see you! What did this reprobate do to get you back?' Santi demanded.

'He faked amnesia,' Emily replied, unable to contain the smile that pulled at her lips from Santi's shocked outrage. An outrage that was perhaps a little too dramatic, making her think he already knew.

'Cabrón!' he exclaimed, punching Javier not so lightly on the shoulder. 'What is wrong with you?' he demanded in an award-worthy performance.

'Me? It's…' Javier flicked a glance to the watch on his wrist '…ten-thirty in the morning, Santi. What the hell is wrong with you?'

'Nothing, Casas. Absolutely nothing! *I*,' he exclaimed with dramatic flair, 'have been nominated for an ETTA,' he concluded, mock polishing his nails.

Emily gasped out loud, rushing downstairs to congratulate him. The ETTAs were world-renowned industry awards and only the best of the best were nominated. 'Santi, that's fantastic news!' she cried, embracing him warmly and missing the warning glare that Javier shot over her head at his best friend. 'Where is Mariana?'

'She's coming—she just had to stop at the bakery. The woman cannot pass a *churro* at the moment without eating it. Even the smell, I swear, *amigo*, it drives her *loca*.'

As the two men embraced, Emily felt a flutter in her heart as she remembered how distant she had kept herself from the beautiful couple. Mariana was generous and funny, while Santi's charm was infectious, but Emily had always felt awkward that they'd had to resort to English while she struggled with the new language and, just as she was beginning to get to know them better, Santi's work took them to Australia for a year and she had not seen them since. But now she wished that she'd not held herself back from the easy affection Javier's friends had offered.

Santi grandly placed the already open bottle on the table, turned to Javier and pulled him into an embrace.

'*Mi amigo*, I couldn't have done this without you. If you hadn't…' Santi stuttered, overwhelmed with emotion.

Emily watched as Javier shook off the praise, as she connected Santi's words with what Javier had told her since she'd come back to Spain. Javier had clearly invested a lot of money in Santi's first film and more, a risky move for a twenty-one-year-old, especially one who feared failure. But she could see how important it had been for both men, their bond irrefutable.

She heard Mariana shouting at Santi before she appeared at the doorway and smiled as she translated the accusation of Santi's desertion, just so that he could go and get his drinking buddy. She was at the doorway when she exclaimed at Emily's presence in much the same way as her husband had—and Emily found herself in a warm embrace, pressed up against a *very* pregnant belly.

'Oh, my…' Emily said, her eyes wide and her hands on Mariana's shoulders.

'Twins.'

'No!' she exclaimed in shock. 'When are you due?' she asked, fairly concerned that it was within the next hour.

'Not soon enough. It's all his fault,' Mariana groused affectionately. 'We're never having sex again.'

'Seems to be going around,' she heard Javier growl quietly and Emily couldn't help but laugh, a beautiful, loud peal that lightened her heart so much everyone joined in.

'Congratulations,' she said. 'Can I?'

Mariana grabbed her hands and placed them proudly on her round belly. 'Emily, meet Sara Torres,' she said, moving one hand to the left side of her bump, 'and her brother Óscar *Javier* Torres,' who was on the right.

Goosebumps prickled her skin as she took in the meaning of their son's name and she looked up to catch Javier's gaze on her and Mariana's baby bump.

Emily wanted this. With him. She wanted to be pregnant with his child, to feel herself grow round with their child and the love that increased exponentially. She wanted to get things right with their child—all the things that their parents had got wrong. She wanted to soothe hurts and ease mistakes with their love and what they'd learned about themselves...but she wasn't sure if they *had* learned enough. She wanted so much to make this work, to make their marriage work, but all the will in the world wouldn't amount to anything if they couldn't put the past behind them. Javier's eyes flared in understanding—as if he had sensed her thoughts—the connection acute and heartfelt until Santi severed it, demanding to know where the glasses were.

Javier sat back beneath the umbrella's shade, happy to find respite from the fierce afternoon sun. The table was littered with plates and glasses, bottles and corks, and *churro* crumbs from Mariana's side of the table. She and Emily had their heads bent towards each other, chatting away happily in a mixture of Spanish and English that had taken Javier by surprise.

'That sounds amazing,' Mariana gushed.

'Oh, God, no. It was awful. But the client wanted it, so she got it.'

'A green quartz bath worth…how much, again?'

'One million euros.'

Emily was enthusiastic about her business—talking about it, she came to life, her movements and expressions much more fluid and confident. She took pride in her work, in her company and her ability, in a way that he hadn't seen before. And he was suddenly curious. Curious about what her offices looked like, what her apartment was like. And he felt strangely awkward that, aside from the short, uncomfortable visit to her mother and stepfather, they hadn't spent any time together in England. He had been in such a rush to make their home here, in Frigiliana—away from his mother's house in Madrid, or his uncle in Barcelona, that he hadn't realised how difficult and lonely it had been for her. And that when she had wanted to return to England, even just to see a friend, he hadn't been there.

He fisted the cloth napkin in his hand and became aware of Santi's heavy gaze.

'So she found out that you were faking?' he asked, pinning him with an unsurprised look.

'What? You don't think that I came clean?' Javier demanded.

'Absolutely not.'

'Fair,' he admitted grudgingly. 'It has not been my finest moment, but she gave as good as she got.'

Santi raised an eyebrow in question.

'Did you not see the parrot?' Javier demanded.

'I saw the *cat*,' Santi replied. 'And I hope

to never again,' he said, shivering and crossing himself.

'Diabla is a Sphynx cat and they are very much misunderstood. They happen to be incredibly affectionate,' Javier defended, unaware even then just how much he'd come to appreciate her.

'If you say so,' appeased Santi somewhat wryly. Javier ignored the bait. 'I am glad to see Emily,' Santi pressed on. 'You are always a bit more balanced around her.'

Javier frowned.

'You are my brother,' Santi swore. 'But I have no idea why you didn't go after her when she left.'

'It doesn't matter. She's back now,' Javier replied.

'Is she? For good?'

Javier didn't know the answer to that question. And for the first time in his life he feared that stubbornness alone wouldn't be enough. Thankfully, Santi let the subject drop and proceeded to tell them about his latest project, making them all laugh about the on-set drama from Hollywood's latest A-list celebrity. Mariana caught his eye a few times, always seeing deeper than the surface, but compassion was there as much as love and Javier knew that she wouldn't probe either him or Emily that day. It was enough to have this moment, the pure celebration of what his one true friend had achieved, he decided as he raised another toast to the film that had made them both.

The sound of his phone ringing cut through the moment, Santi exclaiming at the interruption as if it were a travesty. Javier glanced at the number and had marshalled his features by the time Emily looked across the table.

'My apologies. I have to...' He gestured at the phone and walked with it into the house, missing the shadow that passed across Santi's face and what he mouthed to the question in his wife's gaze.

'Mother,' Javier said, trying to keep his tone level despite the way his pulse lurched.

'Where are you?' she demanded, her tone imperious and shrill. Contrary to what one might assume, Renata didn't drink. There had been no warning signs for him growing up, no empty bottles to find, no trace of drugs to detect. All Javier had was the ability to distinguish the tone of her voice. 'Why are you not here with me?'

The needling would only last so long before it turned bitter and vicious. 'I am recuperating from the accident in Frigiliana,' he replied, hating the way his emotions seesawed, the child in him still wanting desperately to pacify his mother, to give her whatever she needed because, unlike his father, Renata had at least stayed. But he'd been fighting that yoke for years now. Rebellion hadn't worked. Emily and his marriage had also been an attempt to escape that, he could see now. He hadn't fabricated his feelings for his wife, but he had pushed them too far too soon.

'Have you not done enough of that yet? I need you here in Madrid.'

'Ma—'

A curse cut right through his word. 'Don't call me that,' she spat.

Javier took a deep breath. 'I am not coming back any time soon, Renata.'

'Don't talk such nonsense. I have an investment opportunity for us to look at.'

Us being a euphemism for herself. Javier wasn't going to give in this time.

'What about Luis? Can't you speak to him?' Javier hoped that her husband could bear even just a little of the brunt of whatever was causing this meltdown.

'Luis? Oh, he's gone. Done.'

Javier pinched the bridge of his nose, pressing as hard as he could against the rapidly forming headache.

'What happened?'

'He was stealing,' Renata hissed. 'Draining

our accounts. That's why I need you to come back. You need to fix this.'

'No.'

There was deadly silence on the other side of the phone line as he processed that he'd said that out loud, his mind distracted by the fact that this was exactly what she'd accused his father of doing.

'Don't be childish, Javier. I'll expect you tomorrow.'

'No,' he said again, furiously trying to temper his anger as too many things were surfacing. All the times he'd given and given and given and he knew now that it would never be enough.

'How dare you? After everything I have given you. You ungrateful, despicable child. The selfishness! Without me, where would you be? Just like your failure of a father, you'd be on the streets. And you think you can throw all my love back in my face? Let me tell you...'

Santi sighed as he placed the last of the plates in the dishwasher, having helped clear the table after lunch. 'I think it's time for us to be making a move, *cariño*,' he said to his wife.

Emily frowned. 'Oh. You don't have to,' she said, trying to keep the disappointment out of her voice. It had been so lovely sharing the afternoon with them, something she'd missed during her last time here.

Smiling sadly, Santi explained, 'Whenever Renata calls and it takes more than two minutes it's never a good sign, Emily. She either wants money or to berate him, or both. Usually both. It is unlikely that Javier will come back out. But when you go to him, be kind?' The question struck her heart and Emily was quick to assure him that she would.

She bid them goodbye, with smiles and sincere promises to call Mariana soon, but the afternoon had lost its glow and Emily's chest ached for the man she had threatened to divorce not eight days ago. Suddenly the past didn't matter so much—or at least it *mattered* more in that she had seen a glimpse into the child that Javier hid within him, the one who had been so affected by his mother's behaviour and his father's abandonment, and she knew the way that knife cut deep.

She went into the house to find Javier staring out at the gorge from the windows in the living area, lost in thoughts only he could know. Perhaps in some way they had both been running from something when they'd married—hoping to find a bit of what they had been denied as children. It didn't make their feelings any less valid, but perhaps it could make her more forgiving of how young they had been when they'd made those choices. Perhaps leaving had meant only that they could use that time to become what they needed to be before returning to each other a little older, perhaps a little wiser, and a lot more secure. The thought soothed something in her, eased her path forward, and her decision was suddenly easy and clear.

But before she could speak of her feelings, before she guided them towards a future she wanted so deeply it scared her, she had to give Javier what he needed in this moment. She took his hand in hers, guiding him round to face her, and met him in the half turn. She placed her palm against his cheek and pressed her other hand against his chest, locking her eyes with his.

'Talk to me?'

She could see it—the desire in him to shut down, to close her out, just like he had done all those years before. But she could also see that he fought it, was struggling with the need to open up to her. That he was trying meant a lot to her, but that he won the battle gave her hope.

'I am done with her.'

CHAPTER TEN

FOR A MOMENT Javier wondered if he had con-
jured Emily from his deepest fantasies. He'd
heard Santi and Mariana leave, knew that they
would understand. Santi had known him long
enough and well enough to know what he was
like after one of Renata's episodes.

But he'd usually managed to hide it from
Emily. For most of their marriage, Renata had
been occupied with husband number three, so
it hadn't been as much of a problem until she
had left him, citing infidelity, nearly a month
before Emily had walked away from Frigiliana without a second glance.

The warmth of Emily's touch anchored him
here with her when all he wanted to do was
howl and rage and burn.

'I am done with her,' Javier repeated with
such vehemence he felt it in his soul. 'She is
not a mother. She is not capable of such love.
There is a selfishness in her that destroys. And

no more. I will give her no more money and no more time.'

No more of me.

There was a fire burning in his words that rent the bonds he felt towards Renata. And while he felt the split down into his soul, Emily's open acceptance, the simplicity of her touch, the innocence of it undid at least some of the damage Renata had caused that day.

'I am sorry.' Her simple words doused the flames his mother had incited.

'It is not your fault,' he dismissed, wanting to hold on to his anger even as Emily's presence soothed, even as her words unravelled his fury.

'I am not taking responsibility. I am offering sympathy and understanding.'

He scrabbled to hold onto the bitterness and the anger, because if he didn't reach for that he would reach for Emily. And even in the grip of madness he knew that the deal he'd made with her was sacrosanct. She was the only good thing he had left and if he lost her...

'You should go,' he told her, trying to turn away from her embrace.

'No.'

'Emily, please. Go. Now,' he commanded, the hold he had on his restraint feather-light and failing.

'I'm not going anywhere,' she said, holding onto him through the storm of feelings that were thick and tangible in the air between them. She rose on her tiptoes and pressed hot, sweet lips to his. 'I don't need any more time, Javi,' she said against his mouth, in between kisses that destroyed him.

Sweetness turned salty and he realised that her tears had slipped between his palm and her cheek. She was crying. For him. And it nearly broke him.

'The deal—' he tried.

'The deal is done. I want to come home,' she begged as she teased his lips open with her tongue. 'Please. Let me come home.'

Shocked, he trembled with the force of his restraint—what she was offering, what he wanted to take, it was almost too much. Her final plea was his undoing and it tore every last shred of his self-control. As if freed from invisible bonds that he'd strained against for far too long, Javier launched forward, sweeping her up into his arms.

Emily's cry of satisfaction was lost in the passionate onslaught that engulfed them both. She wrapped her legs around his waist as he held her high against him, his arms beneath her thighs and his hands fisting her backside. She tore at his shirt, pulling and snapping buttons that went flying across the floor, whilst also trying to take off her own top at the same time. A few short steps had her back pressed against the wall of the living room—a momentary pause in the chaos created by the way he took her mouth. She offered no resistance, her mouth opening to his, wide and welcoming, her tongue beckoning him deeper, harder as it mirrored how he wanted to fill her elsewhere.

The moan of pleasure seeped from her throat into his mouth, catching his arousal in a velvet fist and squeezing. She leaned forward from the wall, the heat between her open legs pressing against the hard length of him. It was madness in his blood, how much he wanted her. Heat crept up from the base of his spine, reaching the back of his neck as his mind flooded with images of what he wanted to do to his wife. *With* his wife. But this raw primal urgency was something new to him and nothing like he'd ever experienced before.

He pulled back to look at Emily—her eyes wide, glazed with an eagerness that only served to goad him.

'Emily—' he begged with his last shred of decency.

'I want you as you are,' she whispered, her words staccato, in between sharp breaths. 'I want you like *this*,' she said, pulling at his shirt.

He didn't know himself like this, but in her eyes he could see that she was asking him to trust her. Trust that *she* knew him enough. It was all it took to break the final thread holding him back. Need coursed through his body in the space of a single heartbeat—wild and untameable by anyone but her. The feral thing that his desire had become demanded and keened his need.

He shifted his hold, letting her slide slowly, carefully, down the length of his body, enjoying the friction of her hips, her breasts, her hands clinging to him until her toes reached the floor.

He turned her in his arms, stepping them even closer to the wall, reaching for her hands and placing them on the wall either side of her, nearly losing control when she backed up against his erection, her head falling back against his shoulder, restless and needy. His curses littered the air as he ran his hands around her ribs and up over breasts that filled his palms to perfection.

Emily pressed against the wall to stop herself from trembling with the need that was a living thing unwinding in her. She was half terrified that it wouldn't be, couldn't be, satiated. It was too much to be contained. She had never wanted like this—this powerfully, this *much*. It consumed her.

Javier's hands cupped her breasts, his thumbs playing with painfully taut nipples, the ache and throb agitating in the most delicious of ways. Her entire body flashed over with heat, prickling and stinging, and Emily thought she might actually lose her mind to this, to *him*, and couldn't bring herself to care.

One hand left her breasts and, embarrassingly, she cried out at the loss. Feverish, she flexed her fingers against the stone wall, grasping nothing but more and more need. Then he pulled her against him and with his free hand he fisted her skirt at her thigh. Inch by inch he raised the material, as if teasing them both, until his fingers reached her skin beneath the bunched cotton. He palmed the back of her thigh, reaching higher and higher, her breath hitching in her chest—as desperate for what he was seeking as he seemed. He found the band of her panties and pulled, a hard jerk that tore the silk from her body in a way that made her hot and wet in a single breath.

The sob flew from her throat as he ran his thumb across her clitoris and down and back, her hips bucking and shaking, aware of the hard length of him pressed against her. Begging words, pleas, some intelligible, some not, fell from her lips but he was ruthless in his pursuit of her orgasm as if he wanted to punish her—*them*—with pleasure alone.

She felt him use her wetness to ease the path his fingers created, to gentle the delicious friction she craved. Her sex ached with the need to be filled by him as her climax climbed higher and higher. Carefully he pinched the bundle of nerves that throbbed and she cried out, her arms collapsing slightly, as he reached around her to brace them both against the wall.

Emily lost herself as a sea of sensation crashed over her in fiery heat and ice-cold shivers. Longing and need and desire ran through her veins, her body overtaken by pure instinctive feeling. She felt every single inch of her impending orgasm, building touch by touch, gasp by gasp, creeping towards her without mercy. Her whole body flushed with expectation and excitement and as her climax nipped at her toes and fingers she held her breath and...drowned in pleasure.

Waves and waves and waves of pleasure, urged on by Javier, who never stopped touching her, never stopped delighting in the orgasm that rolled through her body again and again. Utterly spent, her head fell forward against the wall, thankful for the way his body supported hers, preventing her from falling to the ground.

His hand returned to her thigh and backside, soothing her while causing goosebumps to scatter across her skin and her heart to jerk once more in her chest.

'Javier—'

'Shh… It's okay,' he soothed. 'I've got you.'

She felt him drop downwards and she tried to look around, but he gently slapped her backside and she understood the silent command. Shock and delight raged to life and pulled her back towards another orgasm.

'What—?' Her words were cut off by a cry of shock drenched pleasure.

Palms braced against the wall, Javier had nudged her legs apart and found her with his tongue. 'I can't… I'm not…' Her hapless protest died on her tongue and he laved her, filled her with the most intimate and carnal of kisses. The growl of his own satisfied pleasure vibrated against her core, and he whispered adoring words so at odds with the sinful act. Her breasts pressed into the cool stone, clashing with the heat coursing across her skin, her nipples aching from blessed icy relief.

He pulled her hips back slightly so that she fell even harder against his open mouth, and again she cried out. One hand reached upwards to claim her breast, finding her nipple, and he filled her again with his tongue.

She grabbed the hand that had claimed her breast. Pressing it against the lush roundness he tormented, she pleaded for him, to feel him inside her, to be able to orgasm around him, with him. She thought she'd said it out loud. She hoped she had, but once again that madness drew her and she wasn't sure, until she felt him withdraw and stand from the floor.

'Cariño—'

'Please, Javi.'

She reached behind her, impatient and desperate, grasping the button of trousers strained by the power of his need. A desire-drunk laugh escaped her husband and he batted her hands away, the sound of the zip being drawn down a musical promise.

She felt the heat of him against her back, the shiver of arousal passing from her to him and back again, as he gently pushed her legs wider, angling her where he needed her. Her heart pounded in her throat so hard with expectation she thought it might stop, until he bent his head and whispered indecently erotic descriptions of how she made him feel in her ear as he pushed so deliciously slowly into her from behind.

Her forehead fell against the smooth whitewashed wall as she trembled with the force of her bliss. He didn't stop whispering as he filled her, deeply, so deeply that she didn't know where she stopped and he began and somewhere in her soul she felt as if the indefinable thing that had been missing was suddenly found. She was surrounded by him, covered and possessed by him utterly, and she *revelled* in it, wanting, begging for more.

There was nothing familiar about this primal need coursing through her, verging on obsession. She had turned into a wanton creature—wanting his touch, wanting his words, his body to completely own hers. He began to thrust, slowly at first, bringing sweet sighs and simple pleasure slowly building towards an inconceivable point both out of her reach and worryingly close.

But then his clever fingers delved between her legs and sharp pinpoints of pleasure fired through her, raising goosebumps and uncontrollable shivers across her body. His thrusts became powerful, rapid, hurling her towards yet another orgasm that she wasn't ready for but wanted more than her next breath.

The sounds around them were an erotic cacophony of breathless pants, sweat-soaked skin slapping against sweat-soaked skin, a crescendo of growls and moans and prayers and curses that peaked on a roar as they came together in a soul-shattering moment that broke them into pieces mid-air and reformed them both into something new as they fell back to earth.

Javier was genuinely worried about opening his eyes—concerned that he really had hit his head in the car accident, that all of this was in fact some concussion-induced fantasy.

Bracing himself, he gingerly opened his eyes half an inch and had never been so happy to see that damn ceramic parrot in his entire life. And then Emily turned into his chest, sweeping her arm across it, and pulled herself into his side and he would have sworn on everything he had of value that his heart turned in his chest.

'Shh...' Emily whispered.

'I didn't say anything.'

'You're thinking too loudly,' she insisted.

He shook his head, unable to stop the smile from spreading across his lips. He peered down at her and she scrunched her eyes together. 'I'm sleeping. Stop it.'

But he couldn't. His hands roamed his wife's naked body as if imprinting every inch of her on them, in his mind and into his soul.

'Oh, God, you're insatiable! No more sex,' she cried in mock horror, turning away from him, causing him to laugh so deeply it hurt his ribs. She was warm against his body and he couldn't resist finding the angle where her neck met her shoulder and nuzzled kisses into it.

'I wasn't joking, Javi,' she groused, but moved her head to give him better access. 'And if I don't eat something soon, I might faint. I'm not joking about that either,' she said.

'Don't worry, *esposa*, you will have everything you could ever wish for.'

He got up from the sofa he'd managed to pull them towards with his last coherent thought before that delicious blanket of satiated need had blocked out all else, making sure the throw he'd placed over Emily was enough.

He ran a hand through his hair, refusing to look at the wall where he'd taken her so desperately and so madly in case he grew hard yet again. *Cristo*. Their lovemaking had always been extraordinary, but that had been something altogether different—new—and simply indescribable.

He grabbed his trousers and thrust them on, not bothering to fasten the clasp. He wasn't sure how long they'd stay on anyway, he thought a little smugly. As he pulled leftovers from the fridge—cold meats, tortilla, olives and Manchego—and put them onto a tray he realised he was trying to work out how much longer he could stay away from work.

They'd returned to Madrid for his checkup, where the Chief of Surgery had been more happy than shocked that his memory had miraculously returned. Javier had been given the okay to return to his local doctor for his final checkup, which was in two days. But beyond that?

He was surprised to find that the driving urge that had ridden him like a demon for so much of his life was strangely absent. He hadn't really noticed it until that moment. He'd not thought of work beyond a few emails that his assistant had forwarded requiring his input or authorisation. He'd received only one phone call from Aleksander, regarding the next meeting of the exclusive and highly secretive charitable organisation he was part of. The King of Svardia had assured Javier that the event in Öström would run smoothly in his absence.

He smiled, wondering what Emily would make of the fact that he now rubbed shoulders with Kings and billionaires alike. So much had changed in six years, but they were still bound by the same thing that had brought them together in the first place. He was *sure* of it. Which was why he turned back to the idea that had needled its way into his post-orgasmic blackout.

He could definitely make it work. And fairly easily too, he figured, as he mentally sorted through what projects he had on the go and where they were at development-wise. In this instance he'd only need a couple more weeks off if he wanted to execute his plan. But the desire to think longer term was pulling at the edges of his mind.

Dusk had fallen, the moon rising into an attractive blue-grey sky, and stars were inking their way onto the canvas above the patio, but there was still half a bottle of champagne in the ice bucket tucked under the table, protecting it from the earlier heat.

He retrieved two clean glasses from the kitchen before returning to the patio, happy to find Emily leaning against the railings looking out at the gorge. The ends of her hair were a little damp from the shower she had taken. She was dressed in his shirt, which was far too big for her and covered all the things that would tempt him to take her right back to where they had been only an hour earlier. Even just the thought of it pulsed through him, hardening an arousal that was still shockingly swift and intense.

Raw. Primal.

There had always been a sense of that insatiability between them, but never so...*carnal*. It had surprised him at first. He'd been fearful of intimidating Emily, shocking her, but instead she'd welcomed it, matched it, demanded it and more from him and he'd gloried in it. And more than a little of him was ready to indulge in her all over again.

As if sensing his thoughts, Emily cut him a narrow-eyed gaze and he shrugged and smiled. 'This is what you do to me, *cariño*.'

He paused only to pour them each a glass of champagne before joining her. He couldn't help but press a kiss to the juncture of her neck and shoulder, his chest mere inches away from her back in a chaste imitation of what had passed before, and offered her a glass.

'Now it is you who are thinking too loudly,' he chided. 'Care to share?'

Emily took the glass he offered, her gaze catching on the deep brown of his eyes, delighting in the invitation she found there.

'I was thinking about how much I want this to last.'

'Then let's make it last. Come away with me?'

'Away?' she repeated, buying time to cover the fact that he had misinterpreted her meaning. She hadn't changed her mind. She really did want to stay, to make a go of it. The thought of divorce turned her stomach and salted her tongue. But she couldn't help but wonder if they were just falling into the same pattern they had before. Rushing into things without taking the time to think them through. Talk things through.

But neither could she ignore how she'd felt seeing Mariana's pregnant belly, bursting with the children she and her husband were bringing into this world. The way she had glowed with the love binding her to Santi and to their future. Envious, Emily had realised that she wanted that so much, because then she might believe that Javier wouldn't one day grow bored of her like her mother had, wouldn't one day find something or someone else to love, leaving her lonely and wondering what she had done wrong all over again.

'Yes,' he said, guiding her over to the table, unaware of her thoughts. He sat without taking his eyes from her and pulled her into his lap. 'I want us to go away. Somewhere we won't be interrupted. Somewhere—' he nuzzled that spot on her neck he couldn't seem to get enough of '—I can do all the things I promised I'd do to you.'

A shiver ran through her body, the pulse at her sex throbbing wantonly all over again. Desire hazed her brain, fogging her mind. 'Where and for how long?' she asked half-heartedly, wondering about her projects and the workload that was racking up in her absence.

'I want to take you to Istanbul.'

Something in her heart turned. He remembered. After all this time, he actually remembered.

'We were supposed to go on our honeymoon,' she said, the words a little sad.

'Santi's movie came up and I had to work to cover the investment,' he said, cupping her cheek and gazing at her solemnly. 'And I regret that bitterly. So, let's do it properly this time. And *extravagantly*!' he said. Effervescent fizz and sparkle filled her bloodstream and a longing so deep and sure Emily was surprised by it. 'We will stay in the finest hotels, travel in the most luxurious style!' he promised dramatically.

'I don't need all that—I just need you,' she said, getting a little lost in the depths of that rich dark brown gaze staring back at her. 'But I'd really love to go to Istanbul,' she said truthfully, thinking—hoping—that she could juggle her workload to make it happen. There was a tendril curling in the back of her mind, unfurling with discomfort, with a wordless warning—but it was so quiet, it was easy to ignore. 'But what about Diabla?' she asked, realising that she was a new responsibility that couldn't be shirked.

Javier frowned and shrugged. 'She comes with us, of course.'

Emily couldn't help but throw her head back and laugh. 'You can't just bring her along,' she said, looking at him as if he'd lost his mind—over a cat that had hissed, spat, scratched and ruined at least six thousand euros' worth of clothing and property in the first two days of her stay here.

'Yes, I can,' he said determinedly. And, just like that, she supposed, yes. He really could.

CHAPTER ELEVEN

THE NEXT FEW days were a whirlwind of activity that struck her almost as frantically as the explosion of feelings and passion between her and Javi. They could hardly keep their hands off each other—and the way that it reminded her of how it had been in the beginning made her feel young and fun and deliriously happy.

Javier brought down his tablet and showed her the plans for their journey. They would take his plane directly to Istanbul. They would stay at a private members' club that he belonged to, once owned by a king, which sat regally on the banks of the Bosphorus. The pictures on the screen showed some of the most opulent, sumptuous luxury Emily had ever seen—a beautifully carved wooden bed, intricate tiling and mosaics that reminded her of the Alhambra, gold, marble and rich deep walnut. Her designer's mind went into overdrive and she had to stop herself from reaching

for the tablet to pore over the images ignit-
ing creative fireworks in her brain. Javier only
laughed, telling her that she'd be there in person soon enough.

They would spend three days there before
travelling on to the Princes' Islands, where
he had leased a sprawling Ottoman villa that
looked more like a palace to Emily. It had staff
and a private chef, and a private beach with
water that looked like liquid turquoise. She'd
never seen anything like it.

Her shock must have shown on her face because Javier asked her if she was okay.

'Javi, seriously. How much money do you
have?'

He studied her, noticing the seriousness in
her tone. 'More than I could ever spend in several lifetimes.'

'More than a billion?'

'Many more.'

'And while we're away, you're just content
to let your billions...do their thing?'

He laughed. 'I have good staff. I trust them.'

'Mmm...' she replied, thinking of how her
call to her own staff had gone that morning.

Javier left shortly after for his final doctor's
appointment, while she remained on the patio,
her hand soothing Diabla's discomfort at the
sudden hive of activity. She smiled as the small

feline butted her head against her palm until Emily picked her up and placed her happily in her lap, because in truth Emily needed the comfort as much as Diabla appeared to.

No, she thought to herself. The phone call with her office manager hadn't gone well. They were happy for her, of course, but she hadn't been prepared for the disappointment. The San Antonio client needed to move up their timescale, which would mean another site visit and condensed deadlines. They were willing to pay, but they wanted *her*. And they wanted her next week. And she couldn't do that. She was making a go of things with Javier, and she wanted their honeymoon. Wanted to explore all the richness that Istanbul had to offer. Her creativity, half-starved until she'd returned to Frigiliana, was ravenous now. At least that was what Emily kept telling herself. It was her creativity she wanted to feed, and to give her marriage to Javier the time and work it deserved.

So she was willing to sacrifice the San Antonio client, telling herself that she and her staff had already been stretched thin and that it was best to give their existing clients their focus rather than splitting it further. And while her office manager had tried to talk her round, Emily stayed firm. She was doing what she needed to do for herself and for her marriage.

Even if it left her feeling a level of discomfort that was strangely familiar.

Diabla flicked her tail against Emily's legs in a syncopated beat that made her smile. The adoring look from the cat as Emily stroked and soothed her was soft comfort that she readily welcomed until Javier came bursting through the front door, declaring to the whole of Frigiliana that he was *free!*

'I have champagne.'

'More?' she asked, laughing.

'I would bathe you in it, if you hadn't taken out the bath six years ago.'

'It was the right move.'

'And yet I still miss it.'

'You have a pool!'

'I do not *wash* in my pool,' he said, mock outrage in his tone as he reached for her, dislodging Diabla, and pulled her into his arms for a kiss that went from welcome to wanton in seconds.

'As much as I would love to take this to its very logical and incredibly tempting conclusion, we must get ready.'

'Get ready for what?'

'Istanbul, of course. We leave tonight!'

Javier was moving fast. Too fast. But he couldn't escape the feeling that there was something coming. Something *bad*. Not usually a superstitious man, he couldn't shake the belief that if they didn't leave for Istanbul immediately, then whatever dark promise was on the horizon would catch up with them and change their lives irrevocably.

So he couldn't understand why—given that his wife had only come here with a suitcase with two weeks' worth of clothes—it was taking Emily so long to pack. He entered the bedroom to find her holding up a pair of trousers and frowning.

'What is it, *mi reina*?'

She shook her head and looked up at him. 'I don't have the kind of clothes that should be worn where we are going. I can't wear *these* to what was once a palace, Javi,' she said, pulling at her simple linen trousers.

'Darling, you can bring whatever you like. But I don't plan on you wearing much through the entire trip,' he said, ending on a growl that formed at the mere thought of her naked, on silk sheets, skin glazed bronze by the Turkish afternoon sun.

She batted him away. 'Seriously. I could really do with going shopping.'

'I will buy you whatever your heart desires…in *Istanbul*,' he stressed, throwing the pile of clothes from the side of her case into it.

'I can buy my own clothes, Javi,' she said with a little more bite than he'd expected. He could feel her scratch as if Diabla had taken a swipe.

'What is it, *mi amor*?' he asked, gently turning her towards him.

'I just...' she tried. 'I just feel like we're rushing this, Javi,' she admitted awkwardly. 'Do we really need to go tonight? Couldn't we take a little time so that I can, I don't know, get the things I need? Like clothes, toiletries, cat food for Diabla?'

He smoothed back the blonde curtain that had fallen in front of her face as she tried to hide her eyes from him.

'Emily, I picked up the cat food on the way back from the doctor's. But—' he held up a hand to ward off her interruption '—if you want to take the time, we'll take the time,' he said easily. He might have been rushing, but the last thing he wanted to do was cause her hurt.

As if his being reasonable took the wind out of her irritation, she puffed out a breath of air that billowed a strand of her hair. 'I'm being silly,' she said.

'No,' he assured her. 'You're not. I just got caught up in the excitement of it, that's all. I'll cancel the car.'

'No, don't,' she said, stopping his hand from reaching for his phone. 'I want to go. I really do. Let's do it!' she said, and he watched the concern he'd seen in her eyes be replaced with excitement. 'After all, I want my honeymoon,' she teased, pulling him into a kiss with one hand and blindly throwing her clothes into the case with the other. The sound of their laughter dissolved into expressions of pleasure and they ended up keeping the car waiting for at least twenty minutes.

A short while later Javier followed Emily up the steps of his private plane, enjoying the way her satin top was pressed against her body by the wind whipping across the tarmac of the private airfield twenty minutes from Frigiliana. He took off his sunglasses and hooked them into the open neck of his shirt, unable to prevent himself from admiring the shape and tone of his wife's body.

'Stop staring,' she threw over her shoulder and Javier barked out a laugh. Lightness filled his chest and he couldn't contain his happiness as it slipped through his fingers and refilled in his hand as if he were taking fistfuls of sand.

'Never,' he promised her and his heart soared at the answering smile that pulled at Emily's lips. Lips that were still passion-plump from the afternoon's adventures. He invited her to sit as the staff stowed their small luggage, one taking very gentle care of Diabla's carry cage, and prepared for take-off. He retrieved his phone from his jacket pocket and it rang in his hand just as he was about to turn it off.

The only reason he didn't ignore the call was because of the name that flashed up on the screen. He frowned and answered.

'Gabi?'

'Oh, God, Javi.'

'Gabi? Are you okay?'

'No, I'm not. It's Mamá—she's...she's lost it.'

His stomach curled. Never before had his half-sister called him like this.

'What's going on?'

He could hear her taking giant gulps of breath before a sob emerged and then almost nothing but tears and incomprehensible words.

Emily stood, concern etched across her features. 'What's going on?'

'I don't know,' he said, shaking his head. 'It's Gabi. Renata's done something.' He turned his attention back to the phone. 'Gabi? Can you hear me? You need to breathe.'

Emily frowned at the sternness of his tone and gestured for the phone. As he half listened to his wife making gentle reassuring sounds to his sister, he fought the decision he knew he needed to make. He cursed. He should have known his mother wouldn't let their last call go so easily. But if he'd thought for a moment that Gabi would be caught up in the fallout he would have handled things differently.

He searched Emily's gaze, hoping his frustration and apology were enough, even as she nodded her understanding. He turned away, fighting the feeling that he had just messed up in the most fundamental of ways, and went to speak to the pilot about changing their destination to Madrid.

Emily was just as eager to get to Madrid as Javier. Gabi had been incomprehensible and inconsolable—nothing like the contained but gravely concerned young woman she had sat with outside a hospital room just over two weeks ago.

It's my fault. I shouldn't have tried... I shouldn't have done anything.

Gabi's words unfolded in Emily's mind and, no matter what questions she'd asked, she couldn't get Gabi to tell her what she'd tried, what she'd *done*. Javier's calls to his mother were going unanswered, which seemed to drive him into a frighteningly still kind of fury that Emily didn't think was healthy. At

least the flight time was quick. While Emily
secured promises that the air staff would look
after Diabla, Javi arranged for a car to meet
them when they landed and it wasn't long before Emily and Javier were walking down the
private plane's steps towards a tall, uniformed
man wearing sunglasses and with a jaw that to
Emily looked as if it could cut granite.

'Esteban,' Javi greeted, surprise and something close to happiness flashed in his eyes
before it dulled back to dark determination.
'You are well.' It was a statement rather than
a question, and Javier's driver nodded.

'You?'

'I'll let you know when I've spoken to my
mother.'

Nodding with an understanding that surprised Emily, the driver pulled open the door
for them and once they were seated returned
to the driver's seat.

Cocooned in the dark interior of the sleek
vehicle, Emily reached for her husband's hand
and tried to ignore the sting when he shifted
out of her reach.

*He didn't mean it. It's a hard time for him,
so don't be selfish.*

The phrase cut her deep, reminding her
of how she'd felt as her mother had begun to
change, to focus on Steven to the point where

Emily had become near invisible. That familiar guilt and hurt began to rise in her chest as she felt shut-out again. Until he reached for her, taking the hand she'd left on the seat between them, his fingers cool but tight, and she knew how much that had cost him because it was priceless to her. That touch, it anchored her. She couldn't be invisible if he were holding her.

She cast a glance at him, the muscle at his jaw flexing rapidly, tension wound so tight through his body that it must have taken considerable effort not to crush her hand.

'Javier—'

'We're here,' he interrupted as the car turned into the open gates and a driveway that circled around a stone fountain before sweeping in front of a huge Tuscan-style estate. The designer in her quickly categorised the impressive building that must have contained at least twelve bedrooms. The front door was flanked by two tall cypress trees, the pink hue of the painted exterior plaster set off by the black-framed windows glowing as every single light in the house appeared to be switched on. She had never been here before. They few times that they had met with Renata, it had always been 'out', as if Renata hadn't wanted Emily in her home. Which, all considered, was probably correct.

Javier took the steps up to the front door in

quick, angry strides and pounded on the door
as Emily followed more slowly, which was why
she could see Gabi when she opened the door.

She looked terrible. Her eyes were red and
swollen from who knew how many hours of
crying, but it was the hurt and fear in them
that caught Emily the most. Her beautiful
long brown hair hung in messy strands and,
hunched in on herself, she looked small and
so, so vulnerable.

'Where is she?' Javier growled.

Gabi put up her hand to try and stop him,
but Javier pushed past her and stormed into the
house, leaving Emily to gather Gabi into her
arms just as she started to cry again.

'Oh, my love,' Emily said, pulling her into
an embrace and sweeping the hair from her
face. 'What on earth happened?' But Gabi only
shook her head.

The moment that raised voices reached them
in the grand hallway, Gabi ran off towards
them, leaving Emily no choice but to follow.
Hurrying to keep up, Emily found the living
area where Renata, Javier and a man she didn't
know stood facing each other.

Renata jerked her head up and with a look
of such venom it nearly stopped Emily in her
tracks said, 'Get her out of here. I never want
to look at her ever again.'

For a moment Emily thought Renata was talking about her, but quickly realised from Gabi's reaction that her ire was directed at her daughter. Gabi turned and fled straight back into Emily's arms.

'That's rich,' the stranger in the room said, in heavily accented English. 'You send her after me like some Mata Hari and now you want to get rid of her?'

'Why would I want her?' Renata demanded. 'She's no better than a whore.'

Emily couldn't prevent the gasp of shock that escaped at Renata's bitter tirade—the way Gabi had flinched in her arms, it was as if she'd been struck. Whatever was going on here, Gabi didn't need to see or hear it. With a glance at Javier, who nodded his understanding, she drew Gabi back into the hallway, down the steps and into the car, refusing to let go of the young woman in her arms.

'It's not true,' Emily said, reassuring her with words of comfort. 'Your mother is wrong.'

'But she's not,' Gabi whispered through pale lips, and her tears became silent, which was so much worse.

Javier shook with a rage that felt endless.

'This is not how I heard you do business, Casas,' said the stranger. 'This? This is unacceptable. Appalling,' the man said, shaking his head in disgust.

'Who are you?' Javier demanded.

The man—as tall as himself—glanced at Renata and back to him again. 'You don't know?'

'I wouldn't have asked if I did,' Javier growled, just about done with this entire mess.

'Lady, you are crazy,' he said, turning his attention to Renata. 'My lawyers are going to go through everything with a fine toothcomb and when they're done...?' He let the threat hang in the air and Renata seemed to drain of all colour. 'She was trying to sell me shares in your company.'

'You mean Casas Textiles?'

'No. I mean *your* company. She's been using your name to secure business deals for months. As it stands? I already own fifty percent of Casas Textiles.'

The ringing in his ears was a warning of how close he was to losing it. The man—apparently appeased by the shock that must have shown on his face—shook his head in disgust. He took a small white card from his pocket and handed it to Javier.

'I'll be in touch. Looks like you've got some talking to do.' And with that he left.

Without looking at the card, he shoved it into his pocket and turned on Renata.

She was trying to look defiant. In her mind, Javier reasoned, she probably hadn't done anything wrong. After all, she'd always behaved as if whatever was his was hers. He shook his head. She really was mad.

'Don't look at me like that. I am your mother.'

'Only when you want my money. What have you done?'

She shrugged her shoulder and touched a finger to the corner of her lip as if checking her lipstick.

'How could you speak to Gabi like that?' he demanded, unable to suppress the rage vibrating in his heart.

'It is true. She—'

'I don't care what you think she did, or even what she did do. You are *unnatural*,' he spat.

Renata's gaze turned ice-cold—a thing that would have terrified him when he was a child. Even now he fought his reaction to the bitter bite of it.

'How dare you—?'

'Me?' He let out a wild laugh. *'Me?'* He struggled to control his breathing and forced the words from his mouth. 'If this man chooses to press charges, I will not stand in his way.

If there are more "investors" out there I will support them also. As for Gabi? No. You will never see her again. And if you try to contact me, or anyone associated with me I will call the police.'

Renata laughed, high-pitched and painful. 'Don't be so dramatic, Javi.'

'I mean it. For your own sake get some help, Renata.'

Javier turned his back on his mother and stalked through the estate that had never been a happy home, down the stairs—pausing only to grab Gabi's bag with her phone and wallet—and into the car where Emily sat, holding his still sobbing sister. He didn't need to tell Esteban to head back to the airport.

In the silence that filled the back of the car, Gabi's tears wrenched at his heart and no amount of sympathy offered by Emily's gaze could ease the hurt. He had let Renata's behaviour go unchecked, both with the business and his half-sister. Elbow against the car door and hand in a fist, Javier became almost completely motionless until they reached the airstrip. He opened the door before Esteban could reach it and helped Emily and Gabi from the car and into the private jet.

In clipped words he told the pilot to return to the airfield just outside of Frigiliana and entered the cabin, where Emily was covering Gabi with a blanket. She held a finger to her lips and motioned that Gabi had finally fallen asleep.

He looked at the small form of his half-sister, wondering how on earth he could have left her to fend for herself against Renata. He'd been so determined to shore up his business— to make himself such a success that failure wasn't a word that could be put even near him. And he had failed in the most fundamental of ways. His sister, his wife… No more. Mentally he drew a harsh line in the sand and in the quiet hour between take-off, landing and the return to their home in Frigiliana, Javier made plans.

By the time they had Gabi settled in the spare room, the headache that had started in the plane had lessened as, bit by bit, the decisions he made came together to form a cohesive whole. Quietly, he drew Emily outside to the patio, picking up two glasses and a bottle of the white Rioja she loved.

'I am so sorry, *mi reina*,' he whispered, keeping his voice low so as not to wake Gabi. He took her hand. 'I know how much Istanbul means to you, to *us*,' he hastened to clarify.

Emily smiled, easing the concern in his heart. 'It's okay. Gabi needed you, and your mother? Well… I think there's a lot of help that she needs, but not from you. At least, not right now,' she said gently. Javier nodded, so glad that their thinking was joined once again.

He leaned back in the chair, exhaling a long breath and taking in the scattered stars above. The plan, he reminded himself, bending forward again and, leaning his elbows on his thighs and turning her hand in his, he pressed on.

'I'm so glad you understand. Obviously, it's going to take a lot of work—and it will take a while—but moving to Madrid will make it easier, in the short-term and probably the long-term. The first thing I'll do is have my lawyers look through everything,' he pressed on as his mind turned over the order of things to ensure that nothing was left to chance. 'And you'll be able to help Gabi because she's really going to need support. God, I'm so glad you're here,' he said, love and plans clouding his eyes so that he failed to see the impact his words were having on Emily. 'I know that we've been apart and I've made mistakes, but I love you. *Cristos*, I love you. And having you by my side, here in Spain, is exactly what I need right now. I know it will not be easy, but it's the best way to—'

He paused only when Emily pulled her hand

from his, and he finally noticed that she was staring at him in confusion.

'What are you talking about?' she asked.

'Moving to Madrid, of course. Where did you think we would live?'

'I thought we might have a conversation about it first.' She half laughed, but the look in her eyes warned him that she was most definitely *not* laughing.

'But why would we need to talk about it?'

'Because I am your wife, not your cat.'

'Of course you are not my cat, Emily. What is wrong with you?'

'You haven't changed at all,' she accused, getting up from the table and brushing her hair back from her face, scrubbing at her eyes as if trying to wash something out of them. She looked back at him and shook her head. 'This was never going to work. How could I have thought that it would?'

CHAPTER TWELVE

JAVIER WAS LOOKING at her as if she had lost her mind. Perhaps she had, because she couldn't work out how she could have forgotten. Forgotten that *this* was what he was really like.

'What do you mean?' he asked, going impossibly still.

Oh, God, she had given up a lucrative commission for this. For a man who didn't even see how much the world revolved around him.

Her hands started to shake. 'I mean that this...' she gestured, between them '...you and me? Nothing's changed. It's all about you and what you want.'

'No, that's not—'

'What about my company? My business—my *life*—in London?'

For the first time that evening his gaze went blank. 'What about it?'

'Do you expect me to just bring it with me to Madrid? All my London-based staff—are they to come with us too? Or do I just get rid of it, and play nursemaid to your family?'

'That is not fair,' he said, standing up in anger and slashing a hand through the air.

'No,' she admitted, instantly regretting her words. 'Gabi does need help and support and I would never refuse her either. But you seem to think that I have nothing better to do with my time. I have a business that is just as valid as yours,' she said, his scoff enraging her further, '*even* if it does not make as much money as yours do. I can't believe that I turned down a commission for this.' She actually growled, grabbing her skirts instead of the hair she wanted to pull at her head. 'Javier! Don't you see?' she asked, allowing the hurt to enter her tone. 'Can't you see it? All the plans you've made, all the decisions, they're all about you and your family.'

'Emily, you are my wife. They are your family too.' His statement hit her like an accusation.

This was going so terribly wrong. Why did he sound so horribly *reasonable*? Something was building deep within her, emulsifying fear with guilt and hurt with anger. She'd done it again. She'd started to revolve around him. Because… because she *did* love him. She loved him so much that the worst thing about his plans was how much she wanted them. How much she wanted to move to wherever he was, how much she wanted to give everything up to make sure that Gabi was okay. How much she wanted to focus on a family with him. How tempted she was to let go of the company she'd built from the ground up. But fear made her harsh and put words in her mouth she would never have uttered rationally and she lashed out.

'So you would move to England then? You would run your empire from London? Bring Gabi and set up there instead?'

He tried to hold her gaze but he couldn't and when he looked away she knew it was lost. That she wasn't enough to make those sacrifices for.

Javier shook his head, disgust and bitterness in his eyes. 'You were just waiting for this, weren't you? Waiting for any excuse. You have *always* had one foot outside of this marriage, ready to leave when you wanted to. Even six years ago,' he accused. 'You could have talked to me at any point about what you were feeling, but you didn't then, and you're not doing it now—you're walking out on me *again*. There is no honesty here,' he all but spat.

'Honest? You want honest?' She laughed bitterly. 'Tell me, did you once think about my job or my life in London when you made your plans? Did you even think of talking to me about what I wanted from my future? No, you didn't because you're just like—' In shock she pressed her hand against her mouth—horrified by the words that she had only just held back.

'Say it,' he demanded, eyes turned almost black with anger.

'No, I didn't mean—' she struggled, back-pedalling furiously.

'You were going to tell me I was just like my mother.' He shook his head, absolutely nothing in his eyes now. 'Isn't that funny? Well, I guess no one could ever accuse you of being like your mother, because if you *did* love me you could never have said that.'

The hurt passing back and forth between them cut her so deeply that it would leave a scar for ever. 'Javi, this isn't—'

'You can go.' He dismissed her with a flick of his hand towards the door.

She went to him, tried to pull him round to face her, but he was as immovable as stone. 'I'm sorry, Javi, I honestly didn't mean that. You are nothing like her. You never have been.'

She tried to manoeuvre herself round to face him, but he kept shutting her out. 'Javi, you know that was not what I meant. Please. You accused me of not wanting to talk. I'm here, wanting to talk,' she pleaded. And just like that, in the space of less than five minutes they had repeated the entire cycle of their marriage. Passion, commitment, withdrawal, and silence.

She had no idea if he heard her or not, but after a long painful moment she knew she had lost him. The implication was too raw, too hurtful, and the argument with his mother far too recent. Tears filled her eyes, for herself, for Javier, for what they could have had...had he not been right. That she *was* scared. Scared of becoming like her mother—a woman who lost her entire sense of self to someone else.

She was by the front door when she heard his steps in the house behind her and she paused, thinking that maybe he'd call her back. Tell her that they were being silly. That they could start again. But instead he said, 'Esteban will take you to the airfield.' And he closed the door behind her.

Javier sat on the patio steps, head spinning and heart aching as the night passed overhead. Diabla wound her way between his legs, nudging the palm of his hand with her nose and meowing as if in mourning for what they had lost.

What had happened?

He ran through the events of yesterday again and again, trying to work out how he had lost so much in such a short space of time. He didn't know where to start because his mother's awful behaviour dived into Emily's accusations. They had hurled hurts at each other that should never have been said.

Emily had been wrong, he internally raged. He wasn't like his mother...but even he could see that in his determination to *not* be, he had become someone who would not bend, would not deviate from his plans. He'd had to be like that. Because growing up with Renata had meant orbiting around her—revolving around her moods and her whims or else.

But that word—orbit—reminded him of something Emily had said days before. The way she'd described her mother and her stepfather as if he were the sun to her moon. His gut began to curl. It was Emily's fear—he knew that. Losing her sense of self to someone else.

He'd not put the two together before, but now he had made the connection he realised that he *did* know what it felt like to lose himself to someone. He knew Emily's fear as a real thing that had happened to him and the thought that she feared that with him? That Emily feared losing herself to him?

Nausea swelled in his stomach. That he could have made her feel anything like that...

He hadn't known that she'd given up a commission to go to Turkey. But now he had to admit to himself that he *hadn't* thought about Emily's job—the job that made her bright and confident and a power to be reckoned with. He hadn't thought about her life in London when he'd blithely announced that they would move to Madrid. His only excuse was that he'd been so desperate to rectify his mother's mistakes—so determined not to fail, that he'd failed his wife. The one person in his life who he should put first, who he should sacrifice for, not force her to make sacrifices.

He gripped his hair in fisted hands and stayed that way until the sun peeked over the gorge.

'Javi?'

For just a second his heart tricked him into thinking that Emily had come back, but even before his pulse had leaped his brain recognised that it had been Gabi who had called his name.

'Are you okay?' he asked, turning to look at his sister.

'I was going to ask you the same question.'

Choosing not to answer, he checked his watch. 'It's early, what are you doing up?'

'I heard a scratching at the door,' his sister replied, her eyes still puffy and red from the night before. She was holding a blanket around her shoulders, looking the way that he felt, he admitted silently.

He lifted his arm and she came to sit beside him, nestling into his side, and then nearly jumped a mile high when Diabla brushed up against her calf.

'What is *that*?!' she screeched.

'*She* is Diabla,' Javier defended, reaching down to pick up the cat, who looked as if she was either going to run away or destroy the blanket that Gabi had pulled around her. As neither option was preferable, he soothed her with gentle strokes. 'She—'

'Has no hair!'

'—is a Sphynx cat,' he continued. 'They were bred that way and she has been poorly treated in the past and is very affectionate.'

Gabi continued to eye the cat with suspicion until Diabla turned in his arms and reached her paws to his shoulders and cuddled into him adoringly, causing Gabi to *ooh* and *ahh*.

'She was probably looking for Emily,' Javier realised, hoping that the cat wouldn't feel too betrayed by her departure. His heart clenched and Diabla meowed.

'Is she not here?' Gabi looked confused.

Javier grimaced and explained what had happened the night before. He realised that it was the first time that he'd spoken about such personal things with his sister and although it would do nothing to help the tear in his heart, it soothed the edges to say it out loud.

As they talked, Gabi made coffee and gathered a breakfast of sorts and he wondered if she realised how unconsciously nurturing she was being. How someone so soft, warm and loving could have come from their mother was a marvel.

'Will you go after her?' Gabi asked, stroking Diabla, who had now taken up residence on Gabi's lap, purring and dribbling her delight.

Javier looked out across the gorge, giving the answer he'd known the moment she'd left their home. 'No.'

'But why?'

'Because she needs to know her own feelings,' he explained. 'She needs to make the choice herself if she is ever going to come back. And I need her to make that choice,' he realised in that moment. 'I need to know that she's not going to leave me again.' *Like his father had.* 'So if she does come back, we'll both know. All this time,' he confessed, looking at his hands and then back to the gorge, 'I'd been telling myself that she was mine, that she'd come back, that our marriage would work because *I* wanted it to. Now I need Emily to want it.'

'Do you love her?' his sister asked, her eyes shimmering with emotion.

'So damn much it steals my breath and stops my heart.'

Two months later

Walking down the chewing gum dotted London pavement, Emily's teenage tears flashed through her mind. While her office manager brought her up to speed with the client requests from the Jenzes' residential redesign, which included a twenty-seater dining table for their extensive and beautifully boisterous family, Emily saw where she'd fallen on ice walking to school, she saw the bench she'd sat on hoping to calm herself after her mother had missed another school assembly because Steven had needed something, she saw herself waiting after a school trip because her mother had needed to take Steven a work file he'd left at home.

'Are you sure you want to do them back to back? We're doing the furniture presentation for the San Antonio project in the evening. We could schedule the installation for the Jenzes for the following day?'

'No, I want them done together as I want to scout out the Kleins the following day instead.'

'Are you sure, boss? I know we wanted to take on more work, but we don't have to do everything...' His words trailed off into silence as she held her words in. 'I'll put it in the schedule.'

'Good. See you tomorrow,' Emily said, ending the call on her mobile as she stared up at her stepfather's house.

She gritted her teeth, having put off this moment for as long as possible, and rang the doorbell. Something about that little *ding-dong, ding-dong* had always irritated her. As if it had never felt right for her and her mum. Or... not the mum that she'd known from a very long time ago now.

And with a start—as if she'd touched static electricity—Emily realised that her mother had been married to Steven for longer than when it had just been the two of them. And it cracked something inside her—cracked the hope that somehow she'd get her mother back. The woman who had laughed and painted with her fingers, who had cooked and made a mess that had delighted her as a child, the woman who sometimes had leaned into a childish silliness in the most joyful of ways...was not the same woman who answered the door in a camel-coloured cardigan and knee-length skirt on a Sunday.

'Darling,' her mother said, eyes crinkling, the blue bright, until she looked over her shoulder as her husband called out to know who it was. Her mother ignored him momentarily as she ushered Emily over the threshold. 'It's Emily, dear. You remember.'

Emily's brows nearly hit her hairline. Had he forgotten he had a stepdaughter?

Catching the look on her face, her mother whispered, 'That I *told* him about your visit.' Emily followed her mother through to the dining table, where two of the three plates already had food on them.

'I'm sorry, am I late?' Emily said, checking her watch and frowning to see it was only just twelve. She was sure her mother had said—

'No, we had to start early—Steven managed to get a tee time at the course with his friends.'

So they'd started without her. Emily bit her lip. She was an adult, a professional businesswoman, a wife even, but this? This cut her deeper than she knew it should.

'Pass me your plate and I'll serve,' her mother offered and even though the thought of food right now made her almost nauseous, she nodded. Her mother placed roast chicken, potatoes, carrots and peas on her plate as Emily watched Steven pour the last of the gravy onto his own.

'How is work, darling? Are you still doing that project in the city?'

It was an ambiguous enough question and could have referred to any number of now finished projects, but Emily didn't want to fight. She never had. 'Yes. It's going well. How are you both? Have you got plans to go away this summer?'

The banal question would have made Javier laugh. Emily could almost hear him in her mind. *Cariño, you're going to have to do better than that.* But Javier's imaginary response was wrong. She didn't have to do better than that because the question occupied her mother long enough for Emily to watch, really watch Steven.

He'd always had this habit of looking straight ahead. Her mother had once explained that he didn't like eye contact and it was then that Emily had realised how much she did need it. For her it was confirmation that she'd been seen and heard. But now she noticed that he did it with her mother too and something curled in on itself in her heart.

Javier never did that. If they were talking, his focus was on her in ways she felt to the depths of her soul. If they were near each other, his eyes would find hers, his attention would be on her in a way she felt like a physical touch. He might have left her alone for days, weeks even at the worst point of his working life, but she had never felt as invisible as Steven or her mother made her feel.

Watching her mother talk for them both, not seeing how unengaged he was, Emily nearly dropped her fork. How could she have ever thought that what she had with Javier was anything like this?

She'd been so worried about losing herself to him, of becoming like her mother—a shadow of who she had once been—that she'd not seen that Javier was nothing like Steven. And more, Javier would never allow her to lose herself. Javier was so passionate, so dramatic, even in his stillness there was energy, movement. She could never have simply orbited him. Emily could only ever hold on for the ride, she realised. And that was it. It was a journey they had been on together. Yes, Javier might have been self-centred and stubborn, but he was not *selfish*.

There was a generosity to him, not just with his wealth, but attention, friendship, passion…that he was capable of giving all of these things, despite the way that his mother had brought him up, was a miracle. Yes, he was rash and quick to act and made decisions without thinking sometimes, but none of those decisions had been about his wants, but what would be best for Gabi, Emily knew.

If she wanted easy, Emily could still walk away. She had her successful business, she was sure that she would one day meet someone who would be nice, great even. But they would never be Javier. Difficult, moody, stubborn...but brilliant, passionate, powerful. They would fight, probably at least once a day, but they would make love in the most spectacular way. There would be heat and spice and salt and sweetness and there would *never* be a dull one-sided impersonal conversation with their children ever.

Emily realised now that she had never lost herself to Javier. She'd never even been close to it. Instead, he'd been slowly guiding her to where she could know and see herself. And, just like when she was working on a project, she'd felt that *thing* click into place—the thing that held everything together. Love. Real, honest to God, all-consuming, utterly ludicrous and completely undeniable love. One that didn't erase her in the slightest, but instead made her *more*.

'What about you, dear? Any plans for a holiday?'

'Yes.' Emily nodded, putting down her knife and fork. 'I'm going to Spain.'

Diabla pawed at Javier's face, thankfully claws retracted, but she wasn't going to let him rest until she'd been given her breakfast.

He growled. She meowed. He considered it a draw. She hopped out of the way as he threw the bedcovers back and stalked towards the bathroom, despite Diabla's attempts to herd him downstairs towards the kitchen.

'Wait, Diabla,' he ordered.

Standing in front of the mirror as the infernal cat drew a figure of eight between his legs, he noticed that finally the marks of the accident had gone. His skin had returned to a healthy colour, the doctors had given him a clean bill of health. There was only one reason for the hollows under his eyes, the loss of his appetite and the ache in his soul.

He ran a hand through his hair before stepping out of his briefs and beneath the powerful jets of the shower. Before she had left the day before, Gabi had made him promise that he would call Santi or Aleksander—his royal friend from Svardia. Not many knew about their association but in the last month and a half he and Gabi had talked *a lot*.

Focusing on his sister and the damage their mother had inflicted had been one distraction from the pain of Emily's departure. It had become achingly clear that, for all his stubbornness and determined focus on what was ahead of him businesswise, there had been a lot going on that he hadn't seen.

His insistence that Gabi should seek some kind of emotional support had been met with a deal—another that had worked to get beneath his skin. Gabi would only go if he did, so together they had met, once a week, with a young therapist to talk about their mother. Gabi visited her separately as well and she had worked incredibly hard to undo the damage that had snuck unknowingly into their lives.

He had not found it easy. *At all.* In fact, other than not going after his wife, it was probably the hardest thing that Javier had ever done. Opening up, talking about feelings, was something he'd spent years purposefully stifling having learned from Renata that such a thing would only be met with derision or denial. But the counsellor was helping—no, he caught himself and rephrased the thought in his mind—the work *he* was doing with her was helping.

Turning off the shower and shaking the droplets from his head onto Diabla, who launched herself from the bathroom with an indignant cry, he recognised that arranging his businesses in such a way that he could take a six-month sabbatical had been the right thing to do.

Aleksander and their associates at the charitable organisation understood completely. Javier had begun to slowly and quietly downsize many of the other smaller and less important businesses, knowing that he did not need to, nor could he, keep up the punishing pace he'd set himself six years ago. His assistants and managers were seeing to that while he adjusted to life with a new perspective. So much had been tangled with how he had seen Renata and his childhood that he was having to learn and understand new patterns of behaviour as much as his old ones.

And every single day he had to remind himself that he was right not to go after Emily. That it was she who needed to know that if she returned it was because of her feelings, not his. And, he admitted to himself, he needed to know that too.

From downstairs he heard a smash and groaned, wondering what Diabla had managed to destroy now. Grabbing a towel and wrapping it around his waist, he was halfway to his wardrobe when he heard another crash.

It sent a spark of alarm through him as he cautiously made his way to the top of the stairs. There was definitely someone else in the house. Creeping down the stairs, the hairs on the back of his neck raised, he heard a thud coming from the sitting room.

Grabbing a long thin vase he'd never par-

ticularly liked, he raised it behind him, ready
to defend himself and his house against whatever thief had mistakenly thought to steal from
him. They could take the parrot, but everything else was *his*.

The first thing he noticed as he rounded the
corner was that the two lurid fuchsia paintings
had come down from the wall and that one was
on the floor, the other missing. He frowned
and glared at the parrot, until a noise behind
him startled him into action.

As he turned, he swung his arm with the
vase and—

Cristos!

Emily ducked just in time to avoid having
the vase smashed over her head—a yelp of
alarm pierced his ears and strangled his heart.

'What the hell do you think you're doing?'
he roared. 'I could have killed you!'

She curled in on herself, crouched on the
floor. 'I'm sorry. I'm sorry.'

Javier's heart pounded so hard he thought
he might have a heart attack.

'Are you okay?' he demanded, fear coating
his tongue with a thick salty bitterness.

She peered up at him and paled. 'Are you?'

'No, Emily. I am *not* okay.' He turned
away, shaking his head, and put the vase on
the floor, even though he wanted to smash it

against the wall. That he could have hurt her in any way made him nauseous.

No, no, no, no, *no*. This was *not* how it was supposed to go! Emily stood on slightly shaky legs, guilty, awkward and upset. 'I'm so sorry, I just... I wanted to... I wanted to put it back,' she admitted morosely.

She'd wanted to undo all the damage she'd done before he'd come out of hospital. She'd managed to get one of the paintings in the small van she'd hired before Javier had appeared in the living room brandishing that vase she'd never liked much anyway.

Javier collapsed onto the awful banquette seating she'd put in nearly three months ago, wearing nothing but a towel, his hair still damp from the shower.

'Why are you here? I thought you'd still be at work,' she asked, getting her breath back.

'Why?' He frowned as if confused.

'Gabi said...' She trailed off as they both realised at the same time that Gabi had set them up.

Her heart beginning to settle from the fright, she went to sit beside him on the seat, her legs needing the support. Just at that moment Diabla launched herself onto her lap and started to pummel her, with claw sheathed paws. The purring and overexcited dribbling were more soothing to her heart than she could have imagined. Her hands swept around the small cat and she scooped Diabla into a hug, crooning adoring phrases and telling her how much she'd been missed.

She caught Javier looking at her with a raised brow and felt sheepish. Apologising, she put Diabla back down and turned to him.

'I'm sorry.'

'That's okay,' he said with a dismissive wave of his hand. 'I know you didn't mean to surprise me.'

He wouldn't meet her eyes. 'That's not what I meant. I'm *sorry*,' she stressed, trying to catch his gaze.

He clenched his jaw, as if trying to ignore her. How much hurt she must have caused for him to do such a thing.

'I went to see my mother,' she said and waited for him to respond. Eventually he nodded and she took it as a sign to continue. 'It was…' she let out a small sad laugh '…exactly the same as it always is, but for one thing.'

She sensed that stillness that wasn't stillness take over his body. He was listening closely, his attention on her in a way that she suddenly felt as love. Tears pressed against the backs of her eyes. How had it taken her so long to realise this?

'I love you. I love you so much and not even that's enough. You are nothing like Steven and I will never be like my mother. Because of you. Because you wouldn't let me lose myself. You demand all of me whenever I can give it, but that requires me to be here. Not to lose myself like she did, and not to someone as unworthy as Steven. You are everything to me and I am *not* less for it, but *more*. I can't believe that I didn't see that before and I'm sorry that I didn't.'

The words didn't rush out of her, they slowly came, one after the other, so that Javier would know that she meant every single one of them. Because she wanted him to know, needed him to know how much she loved him.

'You are…insufferable,' she explained, the flare of surprise in his eyes making her smile. 'You are, Javier. I love you, but you are a pain in the arse,' she declared. 'You are stubborn. You act without thinking, you decide without asking, and you steamroll ahead before you look. But you are also absolutely and without a doubt the love of my life and I am not the same without you. You are passionate, driven, formidable and I wouldn't change a single thing about you because you are…the half of me that

I didn't know I needed,' she confessed, tears escaping down both cheeks. 'And I love you so much it hurts when I'm not with you.'

Javier stared at her, his face unreadable. She swept away one of her tears, the small candle flame of hope that had kept her going since she'd arrived in Spain flickered in the silence. She bit her lip. There had always been the possibility that she'd come too late, that it might not be enough for her to tell him how she felt. Her heart ached and even then she nodded, accepting that she'd tried. Hoping that he might one day at least remember that he was loved for the man he was, not the man someone wanted him to be.

She stood on shaky legs and nodded to herself as tears clouded her eyes. She turned and stepped towards the door, when his hand snuck out to capture her wrist. She paused, not daring to turn, not daring to hope.

'You say that I am insufferable,' he accused, guiding her round to face him and pulling her to stand between his legs. Looking down at him, she should have held the power, but the reality was that she was utterly in his thrall. 'And you are right. I have been and—truthfully—will in all likelihood continue to be stubborn and selfish—'

'No—'

'Let me finish,' he commanded. 'I...became self-centred out of a need to protect myself, but I am learning that I no longer need that same protection. But I am *still* selfish, because I know that I want all of you. I will take whatever you think you can give me and demand more, because you are *it* for me. You are what makes me make sense, you are what I get up for in the morning and what I want to go to bed to each night. You could leave me a thousand times and I will always wait for you.'

'I will *never* leave you again,' she declared passionately.

'I'm still talking, Emily,' he said gently.

She looked down, biting her lip but utterly unrepentant.

'You were worried about losing yourself? You don't need to. Because you are here,' he said, thumbing his heart. 'Always. Whenever you need to find yourself, you are *here*. I know this because I am in your heart. Whether you will it or not, that is where I am and where I will stay for ever. I love you to distraction, Emily Casas. And if you'll agree to nudge me when I forget myself, when I become too autocratic, or selfish—or too much of a "pain in the arse", then I lay myself at your feet and beg you to stay.' Javier got to his knees, caught her hands in his and said, 'And I promise you will never have to ask or beg to be seen or loved ever again.'

Emily met him on the floor and—knee to knee—she placed kisses on his brow, his cheeks, his lips. 'And you will never have to look for me, because I will never leave your side. I love you, I love you, I love you,' she said, placing more kisses on his brow, his cheeks, his lips. Mouth to mouth, they professed their love until tears met smiles and heartbeats soared with a conviction and love that was simply transformative.

In the weeks that followed they put most of the house back to the way it had once been. The tablecloth left the gorgeous oak handmade table, the paintings in the living room were taken down and used for one of Emily's clients, the curtains so disastrously shredded by Diabla were cut down and made into cushion covers in what Emily declared was a stroke of genius and Javier declared was an abomination.

Emily made living in Spain and working in London a seamless affair, commuting twice a month and travelling to clients around the world when necessary. Her staff had come out to Spain for a week-long event that forged long-lasting friendships and working relationships, during which Javier waited on them all hand

and foot, showing an interest in her staff and projects that practically made him a member of the team.

Javier had a slightly trickier transition to his lighter workload, but settled into it happily when he began to accompany Emily on her business trips. Gabi had come by for a short visit with so much news and so changed it had set Emily's head spinning. But it warmed her heart to see how close the bond had become between the two siblings and another building block in the family forming around her slipped into place.

It saddened her that her mother hadn't yet made it out to Frigiliana, but Emily was trying to focus on the relationship she had with her rather than the one she wanted and, bit by bit, it was hurting less. In Javier's arms and with the promise of his constant love for the rest of her life, Emily found a comfort, happiness and security she hadn't realised she was missing and never, ever needed to ask to be seen or loved again.

EPILOGUE

Four months later...

THE SCENT OF pine filled the spectacular penthouse apartment in Madrid so powerfully Javier had threatened to open a window. Gabi had warned him against it on pain of death, and he only relented when Emily pointed out that Diabla wouldn't survive the fall if she became overly inquisitive.

Although he had wanted to celebrate their first Christmas in Frigiliana, Emily and he had decided that Madrid was much more suitable. It was big enough to house his sister *and* the entire Torres clan, as well as being close to the Puerta del Sol—the best place in the whole of Spain to celebrate New Year's Eve.

Seeing Emily and Gabi occupied in the kitchen, he decided that this was his chance to attend to his last festive secret and turned to leave, only to be smacked in the face by a sprig of mistletoe. *Maldito*, did they not know that the stuff was poisonous? Apparently his little sister didn't much care, if the giggles he could hear from the kitchen were anything to go by.

He looked around, seeing that what had once been a sleek, chrome and black contemporary and technologically advanced haven at the top of one of Madrid's most exclusive skyscrapers was now, thanks to his wife's creative talents, like the inside of Santa's grotto.

Navidad had truly come to their home—red velvet bows, green and gold tinsel and frost-coated glass baubles hung from every possible hook, nook or cranny. A tree that had cost an inconceivable amount of money to get up here brushed the top of the incredibly tall ceiling in the living room, leaving barely any room to put the little silver cat Emily had chosen to top the tree, rather than an angel.

Under the broad branches of the Norwegian Fir were mounds of presents. Some were for Santi, Mariana and their beautiful children Sara and Óscar, who were due to arrive in an hour's time. Some were for Gabi and her unborn baby, Javier having had to promise that he would respect her choice and not interfere in a matter he very much wanted to interfere in.

Many were addressed to his wife—from him, from his sister and even one from Diabla, who also had a few presents of her own under the tree. And no, he didn't care how much Santi teased him, Diabla *did* deserve her gifts.

He'd never really much cared for the festive period, the memories of his mother's past behaviour had always made it a difficult time. But three weeks ago he and Emily had talked a little more about her mother and Steven. Javier had asked if she wanted to invite them to Spain, but Emily had explained how her mother and stepfather would go on their 'cruise at Christmas', leaving her behind. He could see the pain it had caused her and how it had helped to impact their lives in ways no one could have imagined. But that day he'd promised her she would never spend Christmas alone ever again and that this—their first together—would be the very best. Which was why he was sneaking off to his office in order to plan a surprise present for her. One that he was sure would eclipse any other gift.

Her husband was up to something, Emily just knew it. Gabi gave her a smile that told her she suspected exactly the same.

'I think he's trying to out-present you,' she mock whispered.

'He can try,' Emily replied, confident that,

no matter what her husband had managed to wrap, she definitely had the best one for him. She placed ham, chorizo, morcilla and Manchego on a large sharing plate. Lobster, prawns and crab would make up the main course, but even that couldn't take her attention away from the sweet nougat called *turrón* that she had come to crave with a need that was insatiable. She glanced longingly at it, Gabi catching her doing so and frowning for just a second. Before Javier's sister could put two and two together, Emily excused herself and went in search of her husband.

Moving as quietly as possible, she turned the handle on the office door and peered through the small gap, realising her error the moment that Diabla meowed, squeezed herself through the sliver of space and rushed towards her favourite human.

Javier turned in shock, quickly trying to cover the half-wrapped present on the table in front of him.

'What are you doing in here? I thought Gabi was helping you with the *entremeses*?'

'She is,' Emily replied, looking at the handsome man staring back at her. He always took her breath away. The rich deep longing she saw in his eyes reflected her own, it was addictive that look.

She pulled him round to face her in the chair and straddled him, much to his surprise and delight. '*Esposa*, we don't have time...' he complained, clearly torn between propriety and desire.

'Really, husband? All your shocking talents and you don't have time for this?' she asked, pressing herself against the hardness of his arousal.

Red slashes brushed across cheekbones that were the envy of many a person as he gripped a fistful of blonde hair at her nape and gently pulled her head back so that he could feast upon her lips. She groaned into his mouth, uncaring of the lipstick she had spent so much time on.

Turrón wasn't her only craving that had become insatiable in the last two months.

Slowing the kiss much too soon for her liking, Javier gently leaned back and levelled her with a searching look. Eyes narrowed, focus intent, it wouldn't take him much longer to work it out. '*Cariño*? What secret are you trying to keep this time?' he asked, his gaze confused, but—she was relieved to see—not hurt. Because he knew that there were no more lies between them now. Only joy and happiness and hope for a future she was excited to meet.

'Just one,' she teased gently, taking his hand

and placing it low on her abdomen where the most precious of all Christmas presents would be making an appearance in about seven months' time.

Javier's eyes grew so wide and so round Emily couldn't help but laugh.

'No!' he said, as if too worried that he might be wrong.

'Yes,' she confirmed.

'Really?'

'Really,' she promised, and then squealed as he picked her up, stood from the chair and spun her round in his arms as Diabla danced between his feet.

'That's it. I'm never competing with you again. You don't play fair,' he complained after kissing even more of her lipstick from her lips.

'No,' she replied, reaching up with her thumb to wipe off the hint of red on his bottom lip. 'I play to win.'

But she was surprised when he looked so happy with her reply. When she asked why, he replied, '*Mi amor*, when you win, we both win, and I wouldn't have it any other way.'

Santi and Mariana and the children arrived then, interrupting a kiss that would have led to so much more if left to their own devices, but Javier and Emily were happy to see them.

Later that evening Emily looked at the people sitting at the dinner table and realised that they were her family. Bonds formed by friendship, by choice, beyond blood, had made their family strong and powerful in a way that nothing else could. And there, in the candlelight, the magic of *Navidad* surrounding them, she looked at her husband and knew that this was the first of many Christmases to come that neither would ever forget.

* * * * *

Head over heels for
The Wife the Spaniard Never Forgot?
Then you're sure to get lost in these other stories by Pippa Roscoe!

From One Night to Desert Queen
The Greek Secret She Carries
Snowbound with His Forbidden Princess
Stolen from Her Royal Wedding
Claimed to Save His Crown

Available now!